SWEET MALICE

KALI SWEET URBAN FANTASY SERIES

MISTY EVANS

Beach
Path
Publishing
LLC

Sweet Malice, Kali Sweet Book 5

Copyright © 2025 Misty Evans

ISBN: 978-1-964028-18-7

Cover by Fanderclai Design

Formatting by Beach Path Publishing, LLC

1

Sometimes, it doesn't pay to be a model employee.

In my case, you show up on your first day of work and end up stuck outside The Gates of Hell because no one is there to let you in.

"Ding dong," I yelled, eyeing the metal portal that exuded enough evil heat I could feel it on my face. There was no doorbell or security monitor. I'd expected a guard to keep out the riffraff, although it wasn't exactly a vacation destination.

I should be able to waltz right in. I'm a demon, after all. Seems like I'd have easy access. Thanks to the Fallen angel who now ruled this place, I was a ghost—able to travel between worlds with nothing more than a thought. The fact I couldn't blow through the gates was...weird. My physical form was more substantial here, though, and not ghost-like at all.

I grabbed one of the horned goat handles. "Anyone home?" I jerked my hand away. "Ouch. What the...?"

It was hotter than, well, Hell, no lie. The skin of my palm sizzled. I blew on it, shook it, cursed.

Beyond the massive gates that disappeared somewhere far, far above my head, tiny bits of ash hung in a supernatural fog so thick it wouldn't let them fall to the ground. Although the dense air prevented me from seeing the ground, I knew it was moving and undulating—a constant shifting of ground, souls, and demons.

I sucked at the burned flesh, now healing thanks to my magic. Every so often, the sound of the undulating earth permeated the fog, and the ground trembled violently as if absorbing the aftershock of a quake.

The earth magic coursing through my body shuddered like I'd stuck my finger in a light socket. The demonic energy rising through my feet and legs tingled. The scent of the scorched landscape trickled through the gates' bars, mixed with the disgusting odor of burnt hair and skin.

"Lucifer!" I'd made it a point to be on time, dammit, and I wasn't happy to be kept waiting. Sliding on gloves to protect my hands, I grabbed the metal bars and tried to rattle them, getting a surge of back-the-hell-off fire that made me yelp. It singed the leather of both palms. "Hey, come on! Are you going to let me in or what?"

As I rubbed my scorched palms together, a figure emerged from the darkness on my left. Height-challenged with a human-ish form bent at the waist, its stringy hair fell over its face. It shuffled toward the gates, smoke puffing from its feet with each step.

Definitely not Lucifer. Still, the magic coming from it made me instinctively move backward. It wasn't a demon, and it wasn't human. Whatever it was, it was dead and headed to the Pit. "Hi, um, are you...you know...going in? Is there like a key card or something?"

The thing lifted its head, nailing me with deep, beady eyes. The skin over the cheeks was wrinkled, the nose bulbous. The mouth opened, revealing rotting teeth. "You do not belong here, demon."

The soft voice was unexpected and suggested a female. Self-preservation firmly in place, I touched my ring fingers to my thumbs, raising my protective shield. "Lucifer is waiting for me. Are you the welcoming committee?"

There was no welcome in her eyes. "It's not your time."

I looked at my watch, now wonky from the magic surge, showing it was a few minutes after two a.m. instead of midnight. "Actually, I'm late now that you've kept me waiting. Lucifer won't be happy about that. If you're the gatekeeper, open these things up."

A prickle of magical needles sliced the back of my arms, my neck. I turned to see a new entity materializing on my right.

"Hecate?" Lucifer strode from the shadows, frowning at the ugly crone. "What are you doing? Why do you look like that?"

"I was on time," I rushed to say, rubbing the prickles from my arms.

The crone morphed, her wrinkles disappearing, her hair becoming a lustrous black, and her physical frame growing taller. Within seconds, she went from caterpillar to butterfly. Goddess energy lashed out and smacked into mine.

"Hecate." Of course. My mother had raised me on stories of Greek gods and goddesses. "Sorry, I should have known."

The now beautiful female quirked her lips ever so

slightly as if smirking at my dullness. "Yes, considering your lineage."

My mother was a demon by nature but was born into a Greek family. She and my father fled the islands and ended up in Italy, changing their last names to Dulce. I only recently learned the whole story about their origins, and I had some profound respect for the goddess before me, seeing as how she'd helped Persephone find her daughter, Demeter. But honestly, I never would have imagined she would be literally standing guard at the gates. It was only a story, right?

Again, I should have known better. My best friend was the Goddess Aphrodite. I'd met a couple of Di's friends, and believe me, they were very real.

"I wanted to see what you would do." Her keen eyes dropped to my ruined gloves as she spoke to my new boss. "Are you sure this is who you want hunting for your brethren?"

Lucifer sniffed. "My choices are limited."

"Hey," I said, although as soon as I saw his face harden, I sucked in a lungful of air and quelled my flippant reply. "I'm here, and I'm damn good at what I do, so can we get on with it?"

Being a three-hundred-year-old vengeance demon who worked for The Bridge Institute for the past few decades to save humans from unscrupulous supernaturals, I had a list of accomplishments and unique experiences on my side. They more than qualified me for this task. Lucifer knew that, yet he hesitated long enough to raise my hackles even more. "While I appreciate your impatience—"

I raised a hand. Surprisingly, he didn't burn it off for my

impertinence. "I prefer *eagerness*. You know I'm every bit as good as Damon at tracking your angel friends, or you wouldn't have traded me for him. Standing here jawing isn't accomplishing that task,"—and we had over one hundred and thirty thousand of them to find—"and I'm sure you have better things to do with your time. Amy and the baby come to mind."

Damon was my boss at the Bridge, and Amy was Lucifer's wife—another Fallen who had been incarnated as a powerful witch. The two of them had a young daughter who was believed to be the most powerful of all—a supernatural who would restore the peace between Heaven and Earth.

Another theory floating around, and that sent most of us demons into fits of unholy panic, was that if God and Lucifer reconciled and humankind was freed of sin, what need would there be for Hell and all of us?

Lucifer was a touchy tyrant and bristled anytime Amy or Azaria's names crossed my tongue. His shoulders stiffened. He motioned at the male hanging around behind him. "Zayfeer will accompany you."

"Your nanny?"

"Manny," the flippant angel said. "Man...nanny... You get the idea. Since Michael is protecting the prize, I have time on my hands."

An angel looking over my shoulder? "Hard pass. I don't work well with others." Especially those sporting wings.

Zayfeer looked about as happy as I was concerning our new partnership. "Yeah, well, I don't work with *your* kind."

"Enough." The word was spoken softly, but its power made my bones tremble. Lucifer locked his steely gaze on me. "You have enjoyed a long working relationship with the Warrior demon, Cole."

"That's different. He's no angel, and yes, he's the best I've found to watch my back. Damon assigned him to me."

"And I'm assigning Zayfeer." The edge to his voice strongly suggested I keep my mouth shut. "Your first assignment is north of Chicago. The address is on your phone."

Zayfeer perked up. "Wisconsin? It's on my bucket list. I love cheese."

Was I in some horrible ripoff of an 80s sitcom? "Where do you want me to bring him or her once I find them?" It was subtle, but using *me* instead of *we* was intentional. I would ditch Zayfeer—I was sure he'd be happy to go off on his cheese tour while I did the hunting—and bag this Fallen on my own.

"That address is also on your phone. You are now renting an apartment near Eden, where you can rest and feed when needed."

Feed? Like I was a vampire? "Aw, you didn't have to do that."

"I did."

Because he didn't want me to hang out here? He wanted to keep me close, but not too close. "Afraid your big brother will use me again to get to you?"

"I have no doubts about that."

Neither did I. The thought of going up against Michael made me swallow hard. I covered it with bravado. "Give me the entire list of Fallen so I won't need to check in between each one. That will only slow me down."

Lucifer was silent for so long, gauging my intentions, I

struggled not to fidget. "No. I want a report of every retrieval in person."

The sitcom had turned into a horror flick. "Perfect. I was just going to suggest that." *Not.* I eyed Zayfeer. "May I speak to you alone, boss?"

Surprise, surprise, Lucifer glanced at Hecate and then at his kid's nanny. "Leave us."

The two of them disappeared, Zayfeer sending me a scowl.

No time like the present to fall on my sword. "Thank you for this."

Nothing I could have said or done would have shocked the king of Hell more. I waited for him to recover and say something, but he didn't.

Go me. I'd rendered Lucifer Morningstar speechless.

"Don't get me wrong," I continued. "Working for you is a —" *Nightmare of epic proportions.* "I mean, I know it's no picnic for you to replace an archdemon like Damon with a lowly one like me, but my friends will be safer with me not there. I had planned to leave the Institute to protect them from your brother, but Cole, Dru, and Rad were onto me."

"Figured that out, did you?" He stood unmoving, his face unreadable.

At least he wasn't smug about it, which surprised me. Lucifer was always smug. "I'm relieved." I'd do anything to keep them out of Michael's clutches, and he currently had a hard-on to make my life, well, Hell, because of how I'd tricked him a few days prior. "I'll do a good job for you."

"Yes, well, I'll throw in a bone to sweeten the pot."

There was that famed smugness. I had a creeping sensation along the back of my neck. Making deals with the devil was a bad idea. *Show no fear.* "Super. What is that?"

He pinned me with knowing eyes. "Do this for me, and I'll release your parents and sister from here."

My gut twisted. I nearly staggered. My family was on the other side of the gates behind him. When I wanted to torture myself, I thought about them. About what they were enduring.

The Devil had turned the tides on me—I was now speechless.

He nodded as if I'd accepted the offer. "Good. Your first Fallen awaits."

Before I could blink, he waved a hand, and I was transported through space.

My ass hit the ground a heartbeat later, sending up a plume of dust. In front of me, a deserted and dilapidated amusement park splayed out like another horror movie scene.

2

*C*lown face signs leered from every abandoned ride and carnival booth. "Hell take me, I hate clowns."

I sat on the side of a hill, frowning at the weed-choked landscape and the scattered rides below, which were in various states of rust and decay. A few tents defied the general apocalypse appearance, standing proud, but their fabric sides were ripped in places, and sections blew in the breeze.

I half expected zombies to appear and was tentatively happy that Zayfeer didn't.

When my sharp hearing caught the sound of footsteps behind me, I vaulted to my feet and whirled. My hand automatically reached for Volante. It came away empty since my whip had been blown to pieces by Michael's former lover, Tabriss. A Fallen angel I hated with a passion, but she was my blood slave now, and I kept her on a short leash. She was never returning to Heaven if I had my say.

A throwing star missed my head by inches as I ducked and rolled, bounding back up and facing my attacker.

"About time you showed up," Cole said. "I've been waiting here for hours."

No whining nanny-angel. In his place, my favorite warrior. Lucifer had the right to be smug. He was intelligent, cunning, drop-dead gorgeous, and held the power of Heaven, even though he was the king of Hell. He'd fooled me again.

If Cole had wanted to hit me with the throwing star, he would have. Missing me showed he cared. I nearly laughed with glee and wanted to throw myself at him, my relief at seeing a familiar face palpable.

Being who I am, emotional displays of affection are off the table. They make me appear weak, and Cole wouldn't appreciate it, anyway. I brushed dust from my leather pants and gave him a cocky smile. "You know archangels, a bunch of holier-than-thou schoolgirls. I had a ton of red tape to cut through."

He approached, picking up the star that I had given him as a gift and pocketing it. "Ready?"

"You're my partner? For real?" Score another surprise for Lucifer's camp. "How?"

His dark brown hair had been shorn close to the scalp. He kept his matching eyes averted. "Damon said you needed someone watching your ass. Last I checked, that's my job."

But only Lucifer got to make that call now. Was he continuing to sweeten the pot to gain my trust? If so, why? "I'm grateful, but I don't technically work for Damon while I'm hunting Fallen."

"I do, and you're my assignment." Seeing my hesitation, he added, "He cleared it with your asshole boss. We good?"

Referring to Lucifer as my asshole boss could get him chucked right into the Pit. Hopefully, Lucifer wasn't listening.

Damon wasn't without his own cunning and ability to manipulate. I knew that firsthand. Had he cut a deal or convinced the devil I'd be more efficient with a tried and true partner by my side?

Right now, I didn't care. I wasn't going to look a gift demon in the mouth. I nodded and strolled a few feet away, brooding. "What are the odds that Azaria will reunite Heaven and Earth?"

He didn't miss a beat. It had probably been on his mind as well. "We placing bets?"

The former Roman gladiator liked to gamble. "Sure, why not?"

"I give her ten to one."

That was more than I'd give. "And if she does? What happens to us?"

He understood I meant the collective 'us,' the demon population. A shrug. "Sin will still exist."

Would it, though? I didn't think so. We tread slowly down the incline, scanning the place for signs of life. "You sound certain of that."

"You're not?"

I stopped midway, feeling my gut tighten. "I suspect there's more to all of this than we realize."

Another shrug as he halted next to me. He appeared casual and relaxed, yet he'd picked up on my sense that something was off. "We're pawns in all of this. Gods, angels, humans...they use us and then exterminate us like ants. That's how it's always been and always will be."

Hunting with Cole was one of my favorite things to do. Still, Michael was out there, crafting some form of revenge on me. That put him in danger. "Are you sure about this? Working with me?"

"No place I'd rather be." He elbowed me, reached under his leather trench coat, and pulled out a fine-looking sword. "I can use some bonus points with the ruler of Hell. Besides, Damon is already making life at the Institute unbearable."

"Why?"

"I have the feeling he's none too happy about your new assignment."

That made two of us. "Why do you want to earn points with Lucifer? Spoiler alert: calling him names isn't your best play."

"Eh, you know. Hedging my bets." I arched a brow, and he grinned. "When you take over Hell, I want to be there."

He always had my back. Always. I never doubted it. We'd been through too much together. "Sorry to disappoint you, but that card is off the table."

"Is it?" He didn't wait for my reply. "Seems like someone has an admirer, even though he'd never admit it."

"What are you talking about?"

"How many demons, or any beings for that matter, have outwitted Lucifer? He doesn't trust you but sees you as his equal in many ways. He dared to go against God; you dared to go against Michael. For him. He respects that. Azaria cleans up the mess he and his witch created, and they live happily ever after. He'll turn over the Pit to you."

I laughed, a full belly chortle that echoed over the empty

park. "Lucifer doesn't see anyone as his equal. And my virtue may prevent me from entering Hell."

Cole held up the sword, light rippling along the blade. "All I'm asking for is a seat at the table when you take over."

"If Hell continues to exist, and Lucifer bails as king, Damon will be in line for that position."

He groaned. "Fuck me."

"Come on, Damon is a prince. He's also got the most experience running large organizations." Which Hell was. "You know what my worst fear is?"

"That Beaumont will write another sappy love song about you?"

Smartass. Rad, my lover, was a former rock star. He'd written plenty of songs about and for me. "Besides that."

"What?"

"That I'm helping Lucifer destroy all of us, along with the humans. Azaria reunites the Fallen with Heaven, returns Earth to Paradise, and therefore eradicates sin for humanity. Without them, we cease to exist."

Fiddling with the sword's handle, he seemed to soak that in. "Then I guess you better start thinking up a plan to save us."

My logic agreed. We stood shoulder to shoulder, gazing down at the ruined park. "What the Hell is a Fallen doing here?" I muttered.

"Beats me." He resumed his descent, sneering at all the clown-themed signs. "As long as there are no actual clowns..." He shuddered.

The prickles along my skin hinted worse things were waiting for us. "I hate them, too, especially *sceleros*." Those were demons that clowns had been based on. We'd recently had one loose in Chicago preying on kids. My buddy, Michael, had used the little prick as a distraction to prime me for his hostile takeover of my vessel, but Rad caught the demon, and I sent him packing back to Hell.

Halting near the entrance to the grounds and a dilapidated sign faded over time, Cole handed me the sword. "Where do we start?"

The weight was just right. I twirled the handle in my palm, jabbed the air in a mock fight, and pivoted to bring it across my imaginary opponent's neck. "Nice. One of yours?"

"I might have taken it off a vamp who didn't need it any longer."

I chuckled. He'd been brawling again. "Let me guess, Dru won't be sending you a Christmas card this year?"

"If he does, I'll shove it up his royal master vampire ass."

"That's the real reason you're here, isn't it? You killed one of the Chicago Undead and pissed off the vamp king. Damon needed to get you out of town until Dru cools off."

"You weren't there, and the guy made a move on my property."

"Brianna is not your property."

"Tell her that."

I rolled my eyes. Cole and the female vampire, who happened to be one of Dru's bodyguards as well as his favorite recurring snack, fought like feral cats and screwed each other like them, too. Most of the time, I couldn't tell if they loved or hated each other. Quite a predicament for a demon such as Cole, who'd lived his whole life killing vampires and knew the female had a thing for her master. Knowing Cole, he probably offed the vamp just to piss Dru off.

I raised the sword so the tip pointed outward, holding it like a water witch using a dousing rod. Sending some of my magic into it, I was pleasantly surprised when it trembled and jerked six inches to the right. "That way."

The blade could never replace Volante but had enough sentience it wanted to please me. We started walking, alert to whatever waited for us. Lucifer may have sent me here, but that didn't ensure there wouldn't be trouble.

Zombies and clowns were the least of our problems when we stopped in front of the funhouse. The building was faded red and without windows. The marquee overhead had lost structural support, and one side listed precariously, ready to fall at the next strong wind. The walls were disintegrating along the foundation, and a swarm of black beetles seethed about the door. We exchanged glances, the sword insisting our quarry was inside.

"I don't like it," Cole said. "Can you sense anything?"

I placed the palm of my hand against the wall, closing my eyes. Earth magic zinged up my legs as I opened myself to it. I held still, enjoying the rush, and tuned my mind to the structure and what it held inside. The beat of a heart came back. So did magic, but it wasn't like ours. It filled my nose with the smell of beeswax, herbs, and blood.

The faint scent of steel registered with the blood—a knife. Sacrifices? Torture? "One entity, but traces of more. Blood magic has been used, but other stuff as well." There was no ward, but bits of spells hung in the air like the ash behind Lucifer's gates. "It feels very...human."

"At least it's not a *scelero*."

"Stay here." I kept the blade at the ready. While I might find more than a Fallen waiting for me, even they could be a handful. Rarely did they realize who and what they were, which caused them to run or fight me. Convincing them I wanted to help was a losing battle. "But stay out of sight."

His hesitation told me he hated this plan. He still did as I asked, slipping into the shadows of the building.

Touching my ring fingers and thumbs together to raise my protective magic, I walked into the dim interior, stepping over the tide of bugs. At least it wasn't rats. I'd forgotten about Lucifer's ring—it reminded me it was present when it heated on my chest.

I drew the chain from under my shirt to find it hanging there. That guy—always thinking about me.

The sigils glowed as if the gold were lit from within with the fires of Hell. I settled the magical passport under my clothes, feeling an odd reassurance that it held protective magic along with its transporter skills.

The temperature in the sunless interior was a few degrees cooler. The odor of unwashed bodies and weed hit my nose, blanketing my earlier psychic smell. My sensitive senses recoiled as I trudged deeper and deeper, using my natural night vision to see.

A buzzing rippled over my skin— magic, and heavy doses of it. Under the putrid surface stink and the ritual odors of burning candles and herbs, I caught another that made me slow my steps. The stench and feel of Lilith, who was technically the mother of all demons, wasn't something you forget once you've come into contact with it.

Definitely not human. Was the queen of demons walking the earth again? If so, how? While logic said it wasn't possible, and this wasn't her usual MO, I knew better than to charge in mindlessly. In the supernatural world, anything is possible.

On high alert, I retraced my steps and found Cole, telling him what I'd sensed.

His face went tight, his magic coiling like an asp ready to strike. "You're sure?"

I'd considered and discarded several possibilities on the way back to him. "Lucifer would know if she was here. Either he sent me into a trap, or it's not her."

"Any hellhounds?"

She always traveled with a pack. They were invisible unless she wanted them to be seen, but I could sense when they were present. "None."

"Could it be a witch like Vicky? Working with Lilith?"

Vicky was a former human witch who was now a vampire and a long-term resident of Bridge's dungeon. She'd once successfully raised Lilith from Hell. "That's my guess."

"Great." He pulled out a dagger. "Can't wait to meet her."

"A witch hiding off the grid in a place like this but forgoing any wards. Weird, right?"

He glanced around, and I knew he was taking in the scenery as if he were human. "I can see some punk kids coming here to do drugs or drink. Maybe a homeless person seeking shelter." Both confirmed the body odor and pot. "Other than that? Maybe she doesn't have anybody to hide from, and this beats paying rent."

"Maybe she's simply human."

"A human dabbling in black magic who doesn't know enough to ward up." He considered it. "Not scared, but seeking something. Retribution?"

It wouldn't be the first time a scorned woman delved into

the dark belly of blood spells to exact revenge. I nodded, yet that didn't feel right, either.

He recognized my hesitation. "Is it possible she already left? That what you're smelling and sensing is residual?"

It wasn't out of the question. "I think we have two different entities." Once, I'd entered a haunted house at a pop-up circus at Halloween, searching for a *lemurea*. Spectral demons attach themselves to buildings, usually houses, where they feed on humans and cause trouble. The more Hollywood versions were actual ghosts and poltergeists. *Lemurea*, however, could appear as three-dimensional as any other creature and often lived and worked side-by-side with humans. They hung around places where large groups gathered, such as apartment buildings, high-rise offices, and the like. The one I'd been hunting fed off the fear people expressed inside the haunted house, adding his own flavor to the ridiculous jump scares.

An amusement park could feed their kind equally well, but with this place being a ghost town, I doubted our magic worker was getting much bang for their buck at this point. Witch or demon, it didn't make sense, but I feared our Fallen angel was their captive. "This building has secret passageways and hidden rooms." Just like the haunted house I'd tracked the *lemurea* through. "I suspect I didn't go deep enough, and when I do, I'll run into some nasty magic. Not only will it try to kill me, but it will alert our current supernatural resident."

"I'm coming with you."

While I didn't want to admit it, I wanted him to. After everything that had happened in the past few weeks, my brain might be the thing that was off in this situation.

Michael had, after all, scrambled it to leave Lucifer a message.

My emotions had also been a roller coaster that could give any amusement park ride a run for its money. "Let's be smart about this, do recon first. I want more intel before we bust in there."

War demons rarely like to cool their heels, but Cole isn't any warrior. He's a bodyguard like none I've ever known. There is no one I would want to go into battle with more. Uncovering information and details about our enemy would mean the difference between a successful mission and being hit with a magical bomb or taking a few rounds of holy water to the chest.

"We're not dying today." He took out a second dagger. "You know the routine. I take lead."

Man, I hated it when he pulled that card, but the training I'd received from him always worked best if I conceded to his uncanny ability to handle dodgy surveillance. Typically, we both preferred to go in guns blazing, but this required stealth.

Don't take it personally. He was better at this stuff than I was, period. "If I get a whiff of Lilith or anything else I don't like, we abandon ship and regroup."

He nodded his agreement. "And if our Fallen is being held against their will?"

He often read my mind. "Their captor is all yours."

He grinned, wicked and evil. I knew which outcome he was hoping for. "Either way, we go for a beer and steak after this."

"I'll buy."

And then I followed him into the funhouse.

3

The sword led us to a room of mirrors. It was round, and we could barely turn around with Cole's bulk.

The door swung shut, and we were in the dark. The mirrors, though, magnified the tiny bit of illumination from one panel. It wasn't light per se; it was a magical glow. We exchanged glances, and the sword trembled when I pointed it toward the spot.

He ran his fingers along the panel's frame, searching for a means to trip it open. "Nothing," he said. "Want me to kick it in?"

"Can you yank off the panel?"

He tried, but it wouldn't budge. Considering his supernatural strength, that solidified the idea that it was enhanced with some pretty hefty magic.

I pivoted in a slow circle, the reflective glass playing havoc with my vision.

"What are you thinking?" he asked.

I closed my eyes, shutting off the contorted and twisted images I was getting from the rebounding glow. I placed a hand against the mirror and opened my earth magic senses again.

Layer upon layer of spells tickled and sliced at my palm. My demon chuckled, amused at the sensations but in no way worried. Probing the layers, I teased and picked my way through several. A brute force attack would have caused them to sound the alarm, but gentle flirting and stroking kept them subdued and curious. "This isn't the way in," I told Cole. "This is just a distraction, a lure."

He rotated to his left, eyeing the other mirrors. "You only need a lure if you're trying to catch something."

I stepped back from the magic-laced panel. "Or trap it."

"We're in a kill box. You can't make a better trap than that."

I reached for the doorknob. "Time to go." It wouldn't turn. No longer willing to be delicate about it, I blasted the locked door with my magic. It swung free.

The stench of sulfur hit my nose before I crossed the threshold. I held up my hand with the sword, signaling Cole not to run out as well as preparing myself for what might come through. "That was too easy. Something is waiting for us."

"Yeah, well, something's already here."

I glanced over my shoulder and saw movement *inside* the mirrors. Each one showed a beast stalking toward us. Hellhounds. "Mirrors are portals. If we stay here, we have to fight them. If we exit, we have to fight what's waiting out there." I pointed the tip of the sword at the shadowy exit. "Your choice."

He gave me that evil, feral grin again. "Why not both?"

As the drooling, skeletal hounds advanced on us with bared teeth, we put our backs to each other. I kept one eye on the exit as I readied the sword to do some damage.

4

We killed six of the eight hellhounds. I was covered in blood and other disgusting things when a figure appeared from out of the shadows and whistled.

The last of the hounds slipped back into their portals and disappeared. Cole and I were breathing hard as we faced the cloaked person who'd called them off.

"I see your first assignment is going well," Zayfeer said. He lowered the hood of his cloak, his angelic eyes glowing in the dim light.

I kept my sword raised, considering if I could get away with slicing him in half and telling Lucifer he was collateral damage during the fight. A glob of hellhound skin and bone slid off the blade and hit the floor with a juicy splat.

He'd be more challenging to kill than the hounds, though. I went on the offensive, anyway. "Where the hell have you been?"

"Good one," he said. "Since Hell is exactly where I've been, and from the looks of it, I'm still there."

Cole wiped his knives on his pants. His demon bristled at the angelic mojo and the snippy comment. "You know this guy?"

"Unfortunately." I used a sleeve to remove blood splatter from my face. "He's my babysitter."

Cole studied one of his blades, turning it back and forth to catch the faint light. "Can I kill him?"

I shrugged. "Fine by me. He's worse than Damon by a long shot."

"Hey," Zayfeer protested. His copper-colored hair was smoothed back in a ponytail. It bobbed with indignation. "You don't even know me."

"You're an angel." Cole stepped toward him. "What's there to know?"

The former nanny had enough sense to back up. "I don't want to be here anymore than you want me here."

I put a hand on Cole's arm. "Any points you make with Lucifer will be forfeit if you kill him."

"You can't kill me," Zayfeer said. "I'm an angel."

Cole chuckled. "Nothing I like better than a challenge."

"You two have fun." I headed out the exit. "I'll go hunt down my target."

Outside, Zayfeer rushed to my side. "If you'd done some research, like I did, you'd know this place is cursed."

I stopped walking. "Cursed by who?"

"Whom," he corrected, glancing over his shoulder at Cole, who stalked him. "And that I'm not sure about, but local legends claim humans go in, and they don't come out. The fairgrounds used to host a yearly Christian revival meeting in the off-season. The last one raised a dozen demons by accident. One possessed the preacher who wiped out over twenty revivalists, including his wife and daughter."

"You don't *accidentally* raise multiple demons." Cole shifted his attention from the nervous angel to the grounds. "One, maybe, two, if you're an idiot. A dozen?"

I nodded. "They opened a portal, and you can't do that without intent and a whole lot of blood sacrifices."

Zayfeer's brows pinched together. "Regardless, the only individual with a heartbeat on these grounds is in the Tunnel of Love." He jutted his pointed chin in the direction of the entrance to what appeared to be an underground ride. "Go get him, tiger."

My last experience with a tunnel had been on my way to break into Vatican City. The memory of the catacombs and their ghosts made my guts crawl. I suppressed a groan. "Why don't you go get him?"

He brushed his hands together. "I've done my part. The rest is all you."

Like all angelic assholes, he shimmered out, leaving us to do the dirty work.

"Think there's still water in it?" I asked, staring at the dark entrance.

"If there is, it's teeming with worse things than hell-hounds." Cole strode toward the entrance. "You want lead this time?"

I chuckled, following. "Is the big, bad War demon scared of water monsters?"

"Hell, yes. Give me fire and brimstone beasts any day, but slippery ones where I can't have my feet on solid ground, and my weapons weigh twice as much?" He made a face. "I hate water fighting."

I did, too. To not drown, I had to remove my cape arsenal, and he was right—maintaining your normal fighting stance and balance was out the window. "It's smart to hide behind a water feature if you're avoiding humans and supernaturals hunting you."

He nodded. "As effective as wards."

The sewer smell emanating from the tunnel caused me to screw up my nose. The pinprick of light sneaking into the opening revealed a stone ramp leading into darkness. I listened for the sound of water but heard none.

Placing a hand on the wall, I felt around for magic or the essence of water. Only a trickle responded. "Since this place has been deserted for so long, the former waterway is dried up. Some rainwater's collected in the basin, but it's not deep."

"And our guest? Is it our witch?"

The sword handle vibrated in my palm. The lack of wards still bothered me. I rolled up the edge of my cape and secured it with magic to keep it out of the stinky water. "Must be, but whoever—whatever—it is, it knows we're here. Tread carefully and watch your back."

I touched my boots with my fingers, sending waterproof magic to cover them. The murky liquid reached my ankles, and I swallowed past the thoughts of all the disgusting bacteria and worse that might be floating in it. I worked with a pestilence demon who had spread some awful diseases in his time. The stories he could tell grossed me the hell out.

The scent of urine and dead rodents made me cover my nose. The trek wasn't long but wound back on itself like a serpent slinking sideways through the terrain. Each time we came to a switchback, I slowed and listened. All I heard was distant calls of crows and occasionally one of the banners or signs banging against a booth or gate when the wind caught them.

At least they weren't hellhounds. With one hand covering my nose, I kept the sword raised. It acted as a weapon to slice through an enemy as well as protection in case they tried to do the same to me.

The enclosure became too dark to see with ordinary eyes, and I used night vision to scan the walls and water. I could feel the heat coming off Cole at my back and knew he was keeping an eye on where we had been so no one could sneak up on us.

A buzzing grew in my ears. I spotted a gunmetal gray steel plate with a green tinge. I took the hand from my nose and made a fist, signaling Cole to stop before I pointed at it. He joined me, knives raised as he continued to stay on alert for any attack as I placed a hand on the metal.

The buzzing grew exponentially, like a thousand bees inside my head. I pulled back and examined the plate, which was big enough to be a door but had no handle to access to open it. Whatever was behind it was being guarded by a strong ward.

Enduring the buzzing, I ran my fingers around the edges, searching for any way to send my magic through and check it out, but there were no gaps.

I motioned for Cole to follow me, and we moved on. Once I was back outside, I could calculate its location and approach it from a different direction.

We made it to the other end with no surprises, but even

after I stepped out of the water, it seemed to cling to my boots. I dried them off in the dead grass as best I could, thankful that my magic kept the water from sinking through the leather.

Cole seemed to feel the same way, grabbing a stuffed animal from one of the old booths and using it to clean his own beefy tactical boots. "That got us nowhere," he complained.

I'd counted my steps from the steel door and the many turns we'd made beyond it. Now, above ground, I backtracked over the landscape, seeing the tunnel below us in my mind. My feet buzzed with its power when I got within a yard of the underground ward. I stopped and pointed down. "We go at it from this direction."

"Using what?" He surveyed the area as if hoping a giant backhoe might appear. "We're not exactly equipped for earthmoving activities."

"Surely the place has a shed full of shovels and lawn equipment."

"Shovels? That's the best you can come up with?"

The sword's tip rose as if pulled by a string and pointed toward a hill in the distance. As far as I could tell, there was no equipment shed there, nor anything else, but I started walking. "Let's see where this leads."

It led us to a limestone wall. Coal shook his head. "I think the sword is defective. I'll have to find you a new one."

"It's not." My teeth started to chatter from the magic coming from the other side of the wall. "This is an illusion. The sword needed to be primed, but this..." I tentatively placed my hand on the wall and felt the sponginess of it. It wasn't limestone; it was magic. "This is our final destination."

"You're sure?" He eyed what appeared to be the wall skeptically. "Can you tell what's behind it?"

"A bizarre mix of spells." That was possibly the reason for the buzzing; each bee was one of the spells cast. Whether it was to confuse anyone who came looking or was simply poor casting on the part of our witch was still up for grabs. "It's both demonic and angelic."

"Another *vitium*?"

I shook my head. "Not possible. There are only seven of us."

"How do you want to tackle it?"

I considered what and who was inside the hill, glancing back to where the underground door was situated. "I don't want to go in alone, but I'm guessing the metal door in the tunnel is an exit. If I spook our target, they might flee."

"Where's that annoying angel when you need him?"

Taunting Zayfeer didn't work. He remained absent. "Guess I'll have to tell Lucifer I need an actual team for these missions." The sword trembled, pointing up. When I followed its tip with my gaze, I discovered Zayfeer sitting at the top. Maybe taunting did work. "Care to join us, or should I explain to your boss why I couldn't snag this Fallen because of you?"

"According to my scorecard," he sneered down at me, "I'm the only one who's done anything productive on this mission. I fail to see what Lucifer needs you for."

"Guard the tunnel exit," Cole barked, "or I'll cut off your wings and feed them to you." He nodded at me and lowered his growl to a level only I could hear. "Let's get this over with. Show him why you're entrusted with this job."

5

*E*arth magic swam up my legs and into my torso. It raced into my chest and down my arm into my hand.

I placed my palm against the spot that looked like limestone and wasn't, closing my eyes and envisioning the charmed ward melting. Demons love to play with fire, and while this was more like lava, it did the trick.

I heard Cole chuckle, and when I opened my eyes, I saw the barrier had disappeared. A lighted tunnel stood before us, much like the one we'd just escaped, leading into a cave.

I glanced back at the war demon. "Ready?"

"Always." He grinned, brandishing both knives. "I'm hungry. Let's get this over with so I can eat."

Come to think of it, my stomach was growling, too. We entered side-by-side, him watching behind us again as I sent my heightened senses ahead.

Unlike the Tunnel of Love, this had no switchbacks and

was short. A few more spelled wards appeared, and I sliced through them with the sword.

We approached a wooden door, arched at the top and custom-fitted into the rocks around it. Not steel, and this one had a handle. It was barely visible amongst the glamour meant to fool human eyes and probably some supernatural ones.

I brushed my hand across it, checking to ensure I didn't get a zap. The voltage was there and strong enough to make me suck in a breath from the slight contact. The sword reacted, and before I realized what it was doing, it sliced at the knob.

The stone didn't give, but the magic did, the ward dissolving into a dozen onyx sparkles that fell to the ground. They turned into wiggling worms that slithered off into the cracks of the surrounding stones.

"That's different," I muttered.

Cole swore. "Beetles, worms...Whoever this weirdo is, they have a thing for bugs."

Not my favorite but not as bad as certain things I'd encountered. "At least it's not rats or clowns."

"Praise Lucifer for that," Cole muttered.

We fist bumped. With every step, my alertness intensified. Ripples of odd magic touched my skin and receded, only to return and recede again. It reminded me of ocean waves but with prickly feelers. After they felt me up the third time, I touched my ring fingers and thumbs together, infusing my field with extra repellent that sent them skittering away.

A glow emanated ahead, suggesting we were nearing our

host's quarters. Rounding a slight bend, I peered through a hazy gloom at another arched opening. The room behind it was crammed with shelves of old texts, a large wooden work table, worn furniture, and a fireplace.

A short, balding man with round spectacles looked up from a dissection plate, a scalpel in hand. "Ah, there you are." He waved me in, the blade flashing under the overhead skylight. The tip was coated in blood, and the specimen on the plate was in too many sections for me to guess what it had been. I suspected from the long, hairless tail that this was why we hadn't seen any rats. "Took longer than I anticipated for you to find me, but I'm sure the wait will be worth it."

A stack of thick books sat on the end of the table, a parchment on the other. A lamp spotlighted the diagram, spots of dried blood and other fluids marring the seemingly brittle paper. "Sorry to keep you waiting," I said, feeling the irritating pulse of odd, mixed-up magics. "Had to stop and play with your pets."

His eyes were brown lumps of coal behind his glasses, flat and emotionless as he removed the rat's intestines, pulling them up to examine them in the light. "You're shorter than I thought you'd be."

I started to say something lippy back, then considered his words. "You were expecting me?"

He dropped the intestines into a glass jar half filled with liquid. They bubbled, smoke rising into the air. He seemed fascinated with it, lowering his head to get a closer view as the acid did its thing. "I've been trying to capture one of you for a long time. Never could quite get the incantation right."

"What the fuck?" Cole murmured next to me.

Placing one of my hands on the nearest stone, I used the other with the sword to block him from charging in. "I can appreciate the whole mad scientist vibe, but here's how this is going to go." My magic streamed into and around the room's walls. I picked up a cacophony of sounds and symbols that had been warded into the space. "I'm going to explain who and what you are, and you won't believe me. Then I'm going to have to prove it. After that, you get to go to a cool place where there'll be a bunch of other beings just like you. You'll be..." *Reformed* was the correct term, but it sounded like brainwashing, and that tended to turn people off. "You'll discover a new life, a better one. You'll have friends."

He snatched up a pen and wrote something in an open notebook before returning to his evisceration. "I'm not a mad scientist." He waved his scalpel around the room. "Frankel Bahar, Demonologist. I thought someone like you would be smart enough to know that I'm not some garden variety schmuck."

"Can we get on with this?" Cole grumbled. "I'm hungry."

I'd lost my appetite but bully for him. "Demon trap," I warned under my breath. "The whole place is steeped in sigils."

"Satan's balls. Why do they always have to make it hard?"

"Thanks for that combination of images you just planted in my head. Now, every time I look at Lucifer, I'm going to either smirk or gag." I began zapping each of the trap's main symbols with my magic. "Be patient. I'm working as fast as I can."

"Come in, come in," Bahar said. "I'm nearly finished here, and then we can have tea and talk."

The grin that stole over his face told me his version of a tea party involved me under his knife. "Have you wondered why you feel compelled to study demons?" I asked, buying time. "Why you don't fit in with normal people? Why you have odd cravings?"

He hesitated for a moment, staring at the blade. "I study your kind because I plan to destroy you. All of you."

The smile he flashed when he glanced up didn't match his announcement.

"That fits, I guess. See, you're actually a Fallen angel, and Lucifer Morningstar sent us to retrieve you so you can hang out with other Fallen and prepare for a big reunion with Heaven." I gave him my best *be a good boy and come along quietly* smile. "Doesn't that sound like fun?"

A muscle twitched under his left eye. "Why don't you come inside, and we'll discuss it?"

Not the response I expected. "You're not surprised by that announcement?"

He returned to his dissection. "He told me you would say something like that. I'm sure it works with most common humans, but I'm not that gullible."

"He? Who's he?"

He pointed at a folded note on the top of a stack of his books with the scalpel. "He left you a message."

"It's a trap," Cole said under his breath. "He wants you to step across the threshold."

I took out the last sigil with my magic and lowered my hand. "Well, I won't be surprised when it doesn't work."

"Kali…" Cole's voice held a warning.

"Don't worry. I've got this."

I sauntered in, enjoying the look of shock on the man's face when I bypassed the pentagram he had on the floor under a worn Persian rug and snatched up the note. Even before I touched it, I could feel the angel mojo radiating off of it. Bahar took several steps back, raising his blade toward me. "You're a demon."

"You seem shocked. I'd almost believe it was real, except you've been raising plenty of us to do your dirty work. And that's why you have this place misspelled—to trap us."

"You shouldn't be able to get this close. The trap should…"

"This isn't my first rodeo. I've been caught in some of those lovely traps, and let me tell you, once you've been in them, you learn how to avoid them at all costs. I've got to hand it to you, though. Yours is intricate, and the layers are a nice touch, but like using the mirrors in the funhouse as portals for hellhounds, I've been there, done that. You can't surprise me."

Cole took a tentative step inside. When he didn't get zapped or trapped, he strode to a shelf and examined a skull. Bahar swung his weapon in Cole's direction. "Put down the knife, asshole," Cole growled. "I don't want to hurt you."

He said it as deadpan as if he was reading a script.

I smirked. "He's lying. He hates angels. But you better do what he says, anyway."

I unfolded the note as the man waved his scalpal back and forth at us, unable to decide who was the biggest threat. The message was short and to the point. My skin crawled. *Say hi to Lucifer.*

It was a trap, after all.

"Get out!" I yelled, whirling. "Michael's been here."

Cole ran for the exit. I grabbed the angel-turned-demonologist and shoved him toward it.

We'd almost made it out when the place exploded.

6

I threw myself on top of the angel I'd come to save. Rocks rained down on me, battering my body. "I stand corrected," I moaned once the dust cleared, blowing a strand of hair out of my face and seeing Cole rise from the debris. "I can be surprised."

"What the hell just happened?" He offered a dirty hand to help me up.

"Michael." On my feet again, I wiped blood off my arm and dust from my pants. "The real trap was his."

"He's the one who left the note?"

I nodded. "Trying to sabotage my mission."

Cole kicked at the man at my feet. His head was twisted at an unnatural angle, and he wasn't breathing. "Looks like it worked."

Some Fallen were immortal; others were not. I suspected the latter with this one, and there was no saving him outside of giving him my blood to resurrect him. That was a moot point— I didn't share blood with anyone these days, even if it meant failing at my assignment.

With Michael behind this little maneuver, it was pointless anyway. He'd chosen an explosion for a reason, realizing it would kill the demonologist. "I knew Michael would come back at me, but I didn't anticipate this."

Cole dug one of his blades out of the rubble. "Not a bad idea—he foils Lucifer's master plan and irritates you." Cole nodded his head as if appreciating the archangel's strategy. Seeing the demon in my eyes, he chuckled. "But I guess he hasn't learned to stop poking the bear."

"He seems to forget that I am, first and foremost, a vengeance demon. For every act like this"—I wiped off the blade of my sword and pointed at the dead man—"he gives me more fuel to seek revenge on his angelic ass."

Zayfeer appeared out of thin air, brows shooting to his hairline when he saw the destruction and our deceased Fallen. "What in the streets of gold happened?"

As if on cue, the folded note floated down out of the air and landed at my feet. It was pristine, untouched by the explosion, thanks to its angelic mojo. I snatched it up and tossed it at Zayfeer. "Michael was here."

He unfolded the paper and read the message. "He purposely killed a Fallen?"

"Well, he didn't use his sword to run the man through, and there's no way to prove it, but yes. Check with your boss and see what he wants us to do with the body."

Zayfeer stared at the demonologist as if willing him to take a breath, sit up, and speak. After a long moment when none of those things occurred, he grumbled in Enochian, the angel language, and frowned. "Lucifer will not be happy about this. I'll be back."

"Make it quick," Cole hollered, even though he'd already disappeared. "I'm hungry."

"Let's search the rubble," I said.

"What are you hoping to find?"

I wasn't sure, but standing around doing nothing wasn't my thing. "Anything that gives me a clue about our victim and his connection to the archangel or Lilith."

"Like what? An angel feather? A signed confession?"

Smart ass. I wiped a layer of dust from my face and stumbled back toward the center of the laboratory. It was now exposed because half the hillside had been blown away. "If only it were that easy."

"How did you know it was going to blow?"

"Just a guess." It was more than that. My connection to the earth had given me a warning. "The amount of hidden sigils in the trap matrix felt off. Like a kid playing with a nuclear bomb. Volatile and on the edge of erupting."

"Impressive the way you disabled the demon trap," he said, joining me.

"A talent Queen Maria taught me when I was fourteen. She liked to subject me to various forms of torture, claiming it made me a stronger and more efficient weapon for her, which I guess it did. After fighting my way out of at least a dozen that she put me in, I developed radar for them."

"Turnabout is fair play, you know."

Queen Maria was a succubus and a *vitium*, like me. Only whatever divine essence she possessed was so tiny that it never made an appearance. If someone could embody pure evil, it was her.

She was now contained in one of the cells in the dungeon under the Bridge Institute, and I had taken the necessary steps to make sure she never got out and hurt anyone again. "You know I can't take revenge for myself."

"Accidents happen. I know plenty of supernaturals, along with myself, who would be happy to mete out justice for you."

Good to know. "I'll think about it."

This seemed to make him happy, a smile crossing his lips. He hopped over a sizable boulder. "What's Michael's endgame? Was he trying to kill us or keep the Fallen out of Lucifer's hands?"

I located the spot where the demonologist's work table had been. It had been blown to smithereens, and I was surprised the man's body was still intact after experiencing such force. "Both?" I kicked through some of the rubble, moving it away from Ground Zero. Unlike a physical bomb, there were no materials to examine, only a charred hole in the ground. It oozed and bubbled a lava-like sludge, and I poked the sword into the foul-smelling substance. The blade trembled in my hand, the metal sizzling in response.

I wanted to take a sample to the Institute and ask Damon if he knew what it was, but I had no container to put it in. Light flashed off some metal on my left, and I pushed a crumbled stone off a small blade—the scalpel. It was still bloody but otherwise unharmed. Picking it up, a jolt of magic hit me, making my teeth snap together. The red-hot material turned black as the night and began undulating in waves.

"Look out," Cole said at the exact moment the sludge morphed into thousands of black beetles.

I tripped over my feet, the ground unsteady as the insects swarmed over my boots and up my legs. As I continued stumbling backward, I dropped the scalpel and swatted at them, swearing and holding in a scream.

Cole didn't fare any better, the beetles covering his lower body. We exchanged a horrifying look and ran as fast as we could from the epicenter.

When we reached the place where the body had been, it was nothing but a shadow outline on the ground. The only thing left was the man's glasses and a watch.

I wasn't one to panic. With my attention distracted by the absence of the demonologist, my brain and magic clicked into place. The beetles clinging to me fell away, dead on the ground from the bolt of my magic. Those racing toward us hit the barrier of my protective bubble and skittered back toward the hole. Whatever hive mind the group possessed, they realized they were going to die, and as one, they blended and merged into a moving black train, disappearing into the hole in the ground.

"What. The. Fuck," Cole yelled, looking down at himself and then at the hole before glaring at me. "Have you ever seen anything like this?"

I hadn't, and I've seen a hell of a lot in my lifetime. "Like I said, it's some weird mix of magics."

"Remember that time we had to hunt down the human kid who was obsessed with ancient texts and trying to make himself a vampire?"

The kid's head had a few screws loose, and he'd thought he could mix and match various ancient magics to create a better version of himself. Problem was, different cultures had unique properties and rules for using magic. He'd created a goulash that backfired. A Frankenstein of power that killed everyone and everything he came into contact with.

Cole and I had labeled him Shelley after the writer who'd written the Frankenstein story. "You think we have another Shelley on our hands?" I asked.

He shrugged. "That's the closest thing I can compare this to."

Zayfeer appeared. "What did you do to the body?"

"We didn't do anything." I held a hand above the dark outline, feeling the same sting of angel mojo the scalpel had given off. "Michael did this."

"Michael took the body?" Zayfeer stared hard at the outline, making a face. "Why?"

I trailed a finger through the shadow, and a zap hit my body, causing my teeth to clench. I drew back. "More importantly, how did he know we were coming after this guy to begin with? Why turn him into..." I poked the tip of the sword at the ground where he'd been. "Whatever this was? He must have assumed we would all die in that blast. Which means he knows we didn't. He didn't want the demonologist talking to us, so boom. He didn't want us to know what he was up to and how he was going about it."

"Now what?" Cole asked.

I headed toward the carnival's gates. "We need a new plan."

"Where are you going?" Zayfeer demanded.

Cole fell into step with me. My insides were turning over on themselves, my mind scattering like the beetles. "We're going to get some food because I can't think on an empty stomach. After that, we're going after the next Fallen on the list." I stopped and looked back at Zayfeer, who stood staring at the shadow on the ground. "Tell Lucifer things are more complicated than I anticipated. I'm going to need substantial backup."

"Why?" Zayfeer asked.

"Because Lucifer has a mole in his organization, my dear angel, and Michael is just getting started."

7

*C*ole and I ended up at a bar and grill. We hit the restrooms to clean up as best we could before ignoring the stares of the patrons and staff and grabbing a booth in the rear.

He'd been my training coach, sparring partner, and friend for so many years that we fell into an easy silence as we consumed copious amounts of food. After three servings of ribs and a side of pasta, I pushed my plate back, unbuttoned the top of my pants, and looked over the dessert menu.

He wiped grease from his fingers and polished off his second order of fries. When I decided on my selection, he took the menu from me and scanned it. "Mission review?"

Most of the time, we reviewed what had happened after such an encounter, along with the outcome, for future reference. We could tweak our approach to the next one by analyzing what had gone right or wrong.

I caught the waitress' eye and signaled her. "I was

dumped on my ass at the fairground, where some ancient evil went down and created a portal." She scurried over, and I ordered the tiramisu while she collected the remnants of our meal. Cole ordered the triple-layer chocolate cake with a side of ice cream, and we waited for her to leave before I resumed. "We fought hellhounds, walked through disgusting sludge, and will probably have nightmares from the plague of beetles that attacked us."

He sucked down the last of his soda. "Plus, we encountered a demon trap, a psycho Fallen, and the ever-lovely St. Michael tried to blow us up."

"Worse than all of that, we lost the package Lucifer sent us after."

"A total cockup. What did we learn?"

He was ever the strategist. "Michael wants to kill us?"

"We already knew that. What else?"

I fiddled with the corner of my napkin. "He got to the first person on our list before we did. Either he's booby-trapped all of the Fallen, or he knew that's where we were headed."

"You're sure he's behind all this?"

"His magic is different than Lucifer's, different than ours. It sets my teeth on edge and beckons me to it simultaneously. It's unlike any other I've encountered and has a unique signature that I recognize. Yes," I said, with a nod, "his brittle magic was all over it. What I can't figure out is why the other magics were as well. I assume the demonologist was experimenting with various ancient powers to raise demons, and maybe he tangled himself up with Lilith."

The waitress returned with our desserts, and we dug in.

"No word from Lucifer yet," Cole said around a mouthful of cake and ice cream. "What do you want to do after this?"

I wanted to return to the Institute and check in with Damon. Pick his brain to ask if he'd encountered anything like this during his stint collecting Fallen.

Zayfeer had seemed genuinely surprised at what had happened, and Lucifer hadn't warned me to be on the lookout for his brother attempting to sabotage any of my missions. It all added up to Michael's new strategy, but he had to have insider information.

Would I find others on my list tainted with his magic? My best bet was to tap into a different resource to learn more about the big, bad archangel. "Let's hit Sweet Investigations. After that, we can pick a random Fallen on the list and track them down."

"What's at Sweet Investigations?"

"Not what, who."

"Aphrodite?"

My goddess friend was working at the Institute these days. I shook my head. "Sophia."

We paid and left a generous tip. In the parking lot, Cole looked over the variety of cars. "Which one should I confiscate?"

I pulled the ring out from under my shirt. We'd walked through the small town of two thousand residents to get here, but I wasn't keen on walking all the way to Chicago. Boosting any of the sad options before us wasn't enticing, either. "Let's try this instead." I grabbed hold of his arm and slipped the ring on my finger. "Sweet Investigations."

A sharp blare sounded in my head, my vision flashed electric blue, and my stomach lurched as I was sucked into a portal. A heartbeat later, Cole and I landed ass over demon balls inside my office. The lights automatically came on, and the wall of screens came to life.

"Welcome home, Kali," my virtual assistant purred in her phone-sex voice. "Hello, Master Cole."

He grinned like the Cheshire cat. "Hello, beautiful."

Sophia, named after the goddess of wisdom, had been programmed by my tech guru, JR, to refer to everyone as master or mistress. I'd requested she not use those monikers, especially with me, but Cole got off on it, so I let it stand with him.

"How may I assist you today?" she asked.

Cole made himself comfortable on the sofa as I took the desk chair. "Give me a list of ideas about what would happen if the archangel Michael teamed up with the mother of demons, Lilith."

There was a long pause before she responded. "The question lacks logic and defies possibility. An archangel cannot perform evil, and a demon cannot perform miracles. Please restate."

Cole chuckled. She wasn't wrong. The likelihood of two such entities working together was impossible when applying the rules of this world with logic. When it came to magic, however, nothing was impossible.

I mentally tried to rephrase the question but couldn't come up with anything in the form that she wanted. My silence prompted her to offer her own suggestion. "Would you like me to create a list of what the archangel is capable of, along with a separate one for the demon, so that you may compare them?"

I didn't think that would answer my questions, but it was a starting point. "Sure. Go for it."

Lists began to form on the two center screens. Cole sat up to read them, and I scanned the lines as quickly as Sophia typed them out. She filled the first with the most common facts about the archangel. Some of those were well-known, but I read a few new ones as the list scrolled by.

Lilith's list was less populated, but what struck me was that both archangel and demon mama had been there at the beginning of humanity.

While both archaic and modern texts placed them in opposite camps and, therefore, made them enemies, they were nonetheless beings directly associated with each other. Their common threads were Lucifer and the Garden of Eden.

Over the next hour, I asked Sophia dozens of rabbit hole questions to see if I could find any other places they intersected. "A scholar of antiquities and lost ancient texts claimed in 1881 that he had uncovered writings in a lost tomb that contained a powerful spell to raise the night bird, commonly referred to and known as Lilith, using an angelic set of symbols originally given to Eve by an archangel." Sophie's voice continued to purr as if she were reading porn to us. "His claims were never verified, the text disappeared, and his body was found crucified in his office. Several scholars he'd spoken to about the discovery claimed the Catholic Church silenced him and stole the document. Their claims were never verified, and the Church denies any involvement."

Easy enough to verify in my mind. "The scholars who spoke out against the Church, what happened to them?"

A brief pause. "One died in an accident, a second committed suicide. The third disappeared on a trip to Jerusalem."

Cole raised a brow. I nodded. Conspiracy theories were entertaining, but I'd tangled enough with Rome and the Holy Catholic Church to know when their fingerprints were all over a denial. "Any chance you can get specifics on that spell?" I asked Sophia.

"There is no known copy of the contents available."

I knew it was a long shot. "Give me a list of any spells to conjure Lilith that use archangel sigils, symbols, or runes that you can find and send them to my phone."

"Yes, Kali. Sending them now."

I stood and headed for the door, Cole following. "You think Michael gave Eve a spell to raise Lilith from Hell?"

Versions of Hell were as plentiful as the cultures that believed in them. I paused and considered that I had a source who'd been there at the creation moment. Picking his brain might yield results but might also end up with me baking in the fiery Pit. "Possibly."

"Why would he do that, and why did she want to? Wasn't Lilith Adam's first wife?"

Good question. "Little is known about Eve, but angels and demons are two sides of the same coin. There are many texts and archaeological findings that have been misinterpreted and re-purposed over and over again. Lilith is another entity that has been built up and dismantled by many cultures under many names, but she was there in the beginning when things went down. While she's typically associated with Satan, a.k.a. Lucifer, who knows what kind of relationship she had with his brother before the whole war of Heaven took place?"

Sophia spoke up. "Kali is correct. The Old Testament was originally written in Hebrew and Aramaic. The New Testament was written in Greek. Each society has evolved, and their stories have been updated to fit the evolving intelligence and cultural norms. Translations are filled with errors and influenced by their authors. Some nuances are mistranslated or changed to suit the author's agenda. All deities have morphed over time or been replaced by others."

"What about asking Salmad?" Cole asked. "He could research his old parchments. Stuff that's never been uploaded to the internet."

It was a solid idea. I pulled out my phone, saw the file Sophia had sent, and texted the priest. When I finished, I randomly chose our next Fallen from Lucifer's list—a couple in Canada. I took Cole's arm and slipped on the ring. "How do you feel about hockey?"

8

*T*he Canadian couple lived in a suburb of Vancouver, a city I'd never visited in my three hundred years. While playing tourist might have been nice, I was tired, keyed up about Michael and Lilith, and had too many others on my list to bring into the fold of Fallen.

Cole bent at the waist, taking a moment to regroup after our spin through nothingness to arrive outside the perimeter of a two-acre dog rescue. The time difference put us at eight in the evening, and through the dusk, I saw a single light inside the farmhouse. Kennels lay to the right, and the entire property was fenced.

However, the gate at the end of the long drive was open, and I began walking up the graveled path. A fine mist fell, layering my face as well as the ground. "Emie and Rachel Horsog, owners and partners of Le Bon Chien Small Dog Rescue and Rehabilitation," I informed Cole.

"Two for one?" he asked, pushing himself upright and following. "They're both Fallen?"

"According to the list."

He scanned the place while I sent out tendrils of magic, searching for signs of angels or demons. The only thing that returned was peaceful night air and the cool earth exhaling as it absorbed the gentle rain.

Before we got three yards from the door, a cacophony of barking erupted from the kennels. A stream of frenzied pint-sized canines raised hell at us and rushed the wire enclosures. An equally loud commotion began inside, and one of the women raised her voice, telling those dogs to settle down.

The porch light came on as I knocked on the wooden door decorated with a grapevine wreath. Next to it, a plaque on the vinyl siding listed the organization's name and founding date, with a brass image of a dog in relief.

A dark-haired gal peeked through the transom side window before unlocking and cracking open the door. "Oui? Are you the Martins?" she asked with a French accent that made her question sound like, *Are you zzzMartins?*

Behind her, the soft glow of a floor lamp spotlighted a dog gate and at least six furry noses pressed against it. One terrier mix with a white mustache and heavy brows jumped on his hind legs, trying to see over the others. He continued barking at a high, ear-splitting pitch.

Having her invite us inside would make things easier, but lying about who we were would backfire in the trust department and make her more resistant to going with us. "We'd like to talk to you about an opportunity," I hedged.

The crack widened a few centimeters. "For zee rescue?"

Not exactly, but this would take all night if I had to get

more creative. "We were hoping to speak with you and your partner. Is she here?"

"Who is it?" A stately female came up behind her, sporting a giant Afro and a brightly colored kaftan. A large gold brooch shaped like a sun weighed down the collar. In the center, a bright blue gem sparkled in the low light.

"We thought we wanted to adopt a big dog," Cole said over my shoulder, "but a recent run-in with some hounds made us change our minds."

Each of them stared hard at us. They didn't quite know if we were lying, but they were naturally trusting souls. The first one opened the door all the way. "You wish to adopt a small dog?"

Looks like lying it is. "Yes," I said. "Small and obedient."

The term obedient made her frown. "I'm not sure if we have anything right for you."

That was assured. I jutted my chin at the brooch, the ice-blue light continuing to draw my attention. "That's beautiful. Where did you get it?"

The change in direction made both of them hesitate. They exchanged a look, and the bearer of the brooch said, "I found it while walking the pack."

Had she? Or had a particular archangel made sure she found it? "It's very unique. I don't think I've seen one quite like that."

Cole threw his arm around my shoulders as if we were involved and squeezed me to him. "Kali loves her jewelry. I know it's late, but we had our hearts set on looking at the dogs tonight."

"Just a moment," the first one said and shut the door in our faces.

Cole released his grip as the sound of their *sotto voce* conversation filtered through the wood, half in French and half in English.

"It's not clowns, bugs, or hellhounds," I murmured, "but it's not going to be any easier."

The dogs fell silent. So did the women. I held my breath, waiting to see if they'd invite us in, try to run, or call the cops.

"Sorry," the first called through the door. I heard the quiet thunk of the deadbolt sliding into the locked position. "We're not right for you. There's another rescue a few towns over. You should check with zhem."

"It's always the hard way," I said under my breath. Motioning Cole to go around to the rear, I raised my voice. "I'm afraid that won't work, Rachel. We're not here for a dog. We're here for you and Emie."

I reeled off my spiel, calculating the police would be here in approximately ten minutes, maybe less. "I don't want to use force," I told them, "but it's imperative you come with us now. You're in danger from the entity who gave you the brooch."

Emie spoke from inside. "He told us you'd say that. Go away. We know who you are, and we don't want anything to do with—"

The back door splintered, and all hell broke loose, dogs barking and the two women screaming. Sending a thread of magic into the lock, I popped it back and entered.

"Don't hurt zee dogs!" Rachel cried as Cole subdued her.

Emie roared in rage and leaped for him as the tiny yapping army at his feet tried to bring him down. I froze the irate female, suspending her mid-jump, but laughed at the fierce attackers tearing at Cole's pant legs and sinking their teeth into his boots. A fat but equally fierce one hung from his arm, its tiny paws scrabbling in the air as it tried to take a chunk out of him. He shot a dose of his magic into Rachel, and her eyes rolled up in her head. She slumped to the ground.

"Get this thing off me," he growled, shaking his arm and the dog.

While he was equally as dangerous as I was, all the dogs, except that one, scattered when I approached. They peeked out from doorways but whimpered and snorted. The one on his arm only growled more menacingly, and again, I couldn't help but laugh. "You can't take care of a five-pound chihuahua?"

"Not without hurting it."

I wasn't sure I could detach it without hurting it, either. I gestured at the couch. "Sit down."

He did, carrying the struggling dog through the air until he could rest her on the cushion. I knelt beside her and stroked the top of her apple-shaped head. "You're exceptionally tough, but now it's time to let go of the nice demon. Can you do that for me?"

She side-eyed me but didn't release him. I massaged her jaws, trying to get them to loosen up. If I sent magic into her, I wasn't sure she could handle it, even at a low dose. "Who's a good girl who's going to release her prey? You've protected Rachel and Emie well. Now you can relax."

She braced her feet on the couch and seemed to sink her teeth deeper. "Ow!" Cole yelped.

Scanning the room, my eyes caught on random toys, but

I went for the bag of treats sitting on a table. I shook the bag as I returned, peeling the top open and waving it around by her nose. Several other dogs hesitantly stepped into the room again, knowing the sound and smell of those treats.

I saw her at war with herself, wanting a treat and unwilling to let go of Cole. "Come on, little doggy. You know you want the treat. It tastes way better than the ugly demon."

Demon blood tastes gross to humans and animals. While she probably didn't understand my words, she did understand the difference between the chicken-flavored treat in the shape of a bone that I pulled out and held in front of her face and the gasoline-tasting blood she was drawing. With a swift action that caught me off guard, she released him and jumped on the biscuit, tearing off into what looked like the bedroom. The herd of dogs looking for their treat tore off after her.

Black blood oozed from the wound, and he used a throw pillow to wipe it off. He sank back on the couch, holding his arm while it healed. "Now what? Can you transport all four of us back to the institute with that ring?"

"I have no idea. Guess we'll give it a try." I looked around at the dogs who were creeping back into the room. The long-haired chihuahua hadn't shared her treat, and they wanted theirs. "What should we do with them?"

"You're asking me?" He stood. "I don't know. Open the doors and let them run free."

A hundred years ago, that's what we would've done. Sure, people had had pets back then, but most had been far less concerned about their care and well-being. "We're evolved, now. We don't turn dogs loose to fend for themselves."

I searched Rachel for a cell phone but didn't find one. Next, I checked Emie. She had one in the pocket of her kaftan. I searched her contacts, finding several labeled 'fosters.' I sent a group text explaining that she and Rachel had to go out of town indefinitely. I needed someone to come and take care of the dogs.

I didn't wait for a reply, setting the phone on the coffee table.

Cole picked up Rachel, and I picked up Emie, drawing the ring on its chain from under my shirt. "Ready?" I asked, managing to hook an arm through his.

"Wait—"

Too late, I felt teeth sink into my leg as we catapulted through time and space.

We landed on our butts inside the perimeter of the Bridge Institute, setting off all the alarms.

Caught in a tangled heap of arms and legs, I cried out at the excruciating pain in my calf, discovering my chihuahua friend had tagged along for the ride.

Cole reached down to haul me to my feet, grinning at our hitchhiker. "Who's a good dog now?" he crooned.

I made a rude gesture, wishing I'd brought those treats with me. The dog would not let go, so I hoofed it over to Emie, removing the brooch from her clothing and pocketing it. She cried over Rachel, who began to wake.

Demons streamed from the building, locked and loaded to take us down, and Cole yelled, "Don't shoot. It's just us. We brought angels."

Aphrodite—Di—and my vampire friend Maddy rushed out, racing past the guards to envelop me in hugs. Di saw the dog and bent down, exclaiming, "You got a dog?"

"It's not staying."

However, it released its clamp on my leg, and she scooped it up. "It certainly is." She nuzzled its face. "You've been through such a trauma. Let's get you inside and get you something to eat."

I swear the dog peered over her shoulder to grin at me.

he institute smells like a typical commercial building, with equal parts carpet, metal, and burnt microwave popcorn. Then, you add top notes of body odor and old coffee.

I took a deep breath and felt my shoulders relax for the first time in days.

I never imagined feeling at home in such a place, but that's exactly what hit me as I passed familiar faces in the hallway on my way to Damon's office.

Word here traveled faster than psychic communication, and Rad ambushed me before I reached the door.

Dressed in distressed jeans and a blue shirt that brought out his eyes, he enveloped me in a bear hug and kissed me hard. Every bone in my body melted, and I welcomed the heat he stoked in my blood.

In the background, Maddy made gagging noises, and Cole coughed. The door of the office flew open, and Damon cleared his throat.

Rad broke the kiss and grinned. "About time you checked in."

"Miss me?" I teased, tugging on a lock of his hair. "Nice shirt."

"Kali," Damon growled in a scolding tone. "My office."

"She got a puppy," Di called, catching up to us.

Damon arched a brow at me.

"It's Cole's," I said, throwing him under the bus.

"Satan's balls," Cole grumbled. "I don't do dogs."

"Why did you have to get a chihuahua?" Maddy gripped. "I hate those little suckers." Her were-cheetah boyfriend had once dated a canine shifter—a cute, spunky chihuahua—to make her jealous. "And dogs hate vamps."

On cue, the dog curled her lip at the teen. "She's a hitch-hiker," I said. "Di will find her a home."

"She already has one." Di hugged her tighter. "Right here with me. What is your name? What if we call you Cutie Pie? No, how about a goddess name? Artemis? Milena?"

The dog barked her approval at the latter.

"We're not running an animal shelter," Damon growled.

The dog wagged her tail at him, smitten with his alpha energy, and gave a cute yip. She liked her males on the dominant side. I didn't blame her. A failing of mine, as well. "We sort of are," I countered. "Of angels."

He glared at me. "Not. The. Same."

"Isn't it?" I quipped, only half kidding. "Dogs, angels. Not much difference."

"You are incorrigible." He opened the door wide and pointed to the visitor seat. "Now."

I gave Rad a quick kiss and sauntered in, my leg already healing from the bite. Damon ordered Cole in with me, and the War demon took the couch as I flopped into the visitor's chair. Damon sat at his desk, scribbling something on a ledger before he slammed it shut and tossed down the pen. "What are you doing here?"

"My job. I brought you two Fallen."

"You're to drop them off and get back to work, not spend time catching up with your friends."

He was often in a bad mood, but I bristled at his lack of appreciation, as well as not inquiring about my health. After all, I'd taken his place with Lucifer so he could return and run the Institute. I'd done him a favor.

"Hey, Kali. Good to see you," I said in my best Damon imitation. "How's it going? The Institute isn't the same without you." I met his challenging stare, reverting back to my normal tone. "Don't overdo it on the welcome back, boss."

He hated it when I called him that. But the look in his eyes told me he was covering for something. Had he actually missed me?

"You wanted to leave to protect your friends from Michael," he grumbled, "so what are you doing in my office?"

"You just ordered us in here."

"Since when do you follow orders?"

Well, wasn't he particularly irascible today? "What's going on? Why are you so upset?"

"Nothing for you to worry about. Do you have something to report or not?"

I shifted so I could pull out the scalpel and brooch. I tossed both on his desk. They glowed with the eerie blue light that was all Michael. "The archangel paid a visit to all of the Fallen on my list so far. He annihilated the first one before I could bring him back here. I don't know what he was planning with the couple I just deposited on your lawn, but he was about to do something because he gave them that brooch."

"Like what?"

"He's trying to sabotage us," Cole said.

I nodded. "How does he know who the Fallen are? Can you look into it? I'd also like to talk to Salmad about a connection between Michael and Lilith."

Curiosity flickered behind Damon's dark eyes. "What type of connection?"

I briefed him about what we'd encountered with the mad scientist. "It reminded me of a kid playing with a chemistry set, mixing a bunch of things together, and seeing what the result is. The only connection between the two may be the demonologist himself, but I suspect there's more to it."

"Michael and Lilith can't be working together," he said.

"We've encountered weirder things."

There was a knock, and I felt angelic energy prickle my spine. Damon called for the entity to enter.

Tabriss was dressed in black, but there was no denying the glowing aura that emanated from her skin. Her hair was done in a fancy braid, probably thanks to Di. She rushed me, dropping to her knees and grabbing my hand. "You are here."

We weren't friends, and her display unnerved me, but I suspected the reason why. "Do you need blood? I thought I left plenty for everyone."

She licked her lips, her eyes lit with fervor. "No, I am satiated. Did you see him?"

"Who?"

A tremulous smile broke across her face. "Michael, of course."

Long ago, in a place called Heaven, the two of them were tight. She was Fallen now, though, and when Michael had discovered she was my blood slave, he'd turned his back on her. "Why would you think I've seen him?"

The leather squeaked as Cole leaned forward. "Do you know what he's up to?"

Her eyes never left my face. "Did he say anything about me?"

I removed my hand from her grip. "I haven't seen or spoken to him. We're in the middle of a meeting. If you know what he's up to, great. Tell us. If not, you need to leave."

Her attention tracked to the items on the desk. "I can sense him." She shifted to kneel before the desk.

Before she could lock her hands on the scalpel and brooch, I snagged her by the collar and hauled her backward. Coming to my feet, I shoved her toward the door. "Get out, Tabriss. Go to your quarters and wait for Damon."

She whirled and punched me in the face, knocking me to the ground.

I cursed and bounded back to my feet, my nose spilling blood, but as she lunged for the items, Cole caught her in a vise grip and pinned her to the wall.

I wiped blood from my upper lip. "What the hell?"

Damon scooped the Michael-imbued artifacts into a drawer. "Take her to the chapel," he ordered. "Have Salmad douse her in holy water."

I wasn't sure why that would help, but at least it would get her out of the proximity of the items. Cole wrestled her from the room, and I watched Damon go to a section of his bookshelves. He pressed an invisible button, and a portion of the shelves slid sideways.

Behind them, a panel opened, revealing a wall safe. He muttered words in a dead language under his breath, which unlocked it. He withdrew a zippered pouch.

Returning to his desk, he slipped the artifacts inside. "This should contain their magic and break their connection to Michael," he said, zipping it.

"You never told me you had a safe in here."

"I haven't needed one until now." He returned the pouch to it and locked it up. "With so many entities residing inside these walls, it seems prudent."

"With so many *Fallen*," I corrected. We had more to worry about from them than any of the demons or other supers living here. "Why drown Tabriss in holy water if that pouch will do the trick of breaking the compulsion?"

He shrugged, giving a faint smile. "No reason."

"You want everyone to believe that's the way it works."

"No one will come sniffing around for the real impetus then."

Smart. "Any idea what game Michael's playing? Is this just about thwarting Lucifer, or does he fear the big divine reunion?"

He returned to his desk, looking as tired as I felt. Mental battles were as taxing as physical ones. "Both." He motioned at the door. "See your friends, talk to Salmad, get some rest. Then get back out there and track down the next Fallen. I have the feeling we're running low on time."

Heading to the chapel, previously an interrogation space the priest had converted for his growing congregation, I turned ideas over in my mind. I preferred efficiency, and hunting down Lucifer's friends would take years at this rate. I sensed the same thing Damon did—we had a limited time-frame with Michael breathing down our necks. Since he was duty-bound to keep Azaria from harm now, he was being more creative in stopping her destiny from coming to fruition.

Salmad was holding a prayer service in the chapel. As I neared the gathering, my skin tingled and itched from the level of angel magic. My ears buzzed, and my teeth ground against each other.

Inside the nave, the group was packed tight, singing a hymn. As one, they swayed. Tabriss was at the front, drenched to the bone. Cole was nowhere in sight.

While humans love to hear angelic voices, to a demon, it's worse than howling hellhounds. I longed for earplugs but had to settle for layering a bit of my magic over my ears as I marched to the front of the group to stand at the foot of the pulpit.

Salmad gave me an irritated shake of his head, warning me not to interrupt.

I did anyway, using a sharp whistle to bring the singing to a stop. "That's all for today," I said loud enough to shut down the last few, which were still carrying on. I clapped my hands and made waving motions. Most of them blinked at me, exchanging looks as if coming out of a trance.

"What is the meaning of this, Kali?" Salmad said through clenched teeth. "This is a sacred space, and you're being rude."

Rude? I chuckled to myself. "Everyone out," I ordered. I

turned to him. "I need to talk to you about something impor-tant involving Michael and Lilith."

"Can't it wait?" He gripped the sides of the pulpit, turning his knuckles white. "It's rare I can get them all together like this."

A few stood and moved toward the exit. I waved at those in the closest rows, shooing them off. "No can do, priest. We need to talk now."

"Let's resume today at two," he called to the exiting congregation. "I'll make sure we're not interrupted at that time."

A few stragglers gave me the evil eye. I gave it right back.

Once we were alone, I told him about my experience with the demonologist and the mixed-up magics. I also filled him in about the artifacts infused with Michael's magic. "I asked Sophia about spells that link him to Lilith or any history I could call on to figure out a potential liaison between them, but she came up mostly blank." I gave him the info that she had shared about the archaeologist and shrugged. "What do you think?"

His face was tight, his eyes still snapping with anger. "I don't know anything off the top of my head that I can tell you, but I'll research it."

I clapped him on the shoulder. "Thanks."

"That's it? You dump that on me and say thanks without an apology for interrupting my gathering?"

"You do understand the importance of my job, right? I'm charged with locating and bringing in thousands of Fallen. Working around other people's schedules is not a high priority for me. Lucifer is an impatient master, and I don't owe you an apology. I need everyone onboard, using their skills and capabilities to help me with this. I'm sorry if I hurt your feelings but get over it. We're not here to be friends with or play nursemaid to these angels. We are here to recover and rehabilitate them before handing them over to the king of Hell."

He blustered, and I left him standing there in his self-righteousness. "As soon as you have anything, call me," I said over my shoulder as I marched out.

The heat in my blood drew me to Rad, who waited in my assigned room. Neither of us said a word, stripping each other of our clothes and coming together in a flurry of desperation and lust.

He swore softly in French as I grabbed him and guided him inside me, my hips bucking against him as my legs locked him into an unbreakable grip. We didn't make it to the bed, and he pinned me to the wall as he drove himself into me over and over again. My climax hit hard and fast, and I cried out, my magic blowing out of me. The gust knocked over the bookcase and sent the contents across the floor.

He slammed a hand into the wall as he followed me into bliss, and it was only a few moments later, as we came down from our lust, that I realized he'd put a hole through the plaster.

Words still escaped us as we fell, laughing, onto the bed. We kissed, and he trailed his hands over my naked body as if he couldn't get enough of me.

Two fingers slipped inside of me, and I gasped, my body quaking again with desire. He lowered his mouth to one of my breasts, and I felt a second orgasm on the verge of exploding between my legs. I sank one hand into his hair, gripping it tight, my body arching under his. The other scratched and clawed at his back.

Just as I was about to go over the cliff of pleasure again, I felt an odd tug in the center of my chest, right below my breastbone. My body became transparent, and Rad swore. "What is going on?"

"Oh, shit." I tried to force him off me, but my hand became spectral, and it went right through his shoulder. I could no longer feel his fingers inside me. "Lucifer is..."

The next instant, I was standing outside the gates of Hell again.

Only this time, I was completely naked, and Lucifer was waiting for me.

10

"*W*hat in the fires of Hell are you doing?"

The condescending tone was as cold as the divine magic rippling off him and sending goosebumps chasing each other over my skin. I would have been an icicle if it hadn't been for the blazing heat oozing through the gates. "I was in the middle of an orgasm. You need to work on your timing."

If what he saw invoked lust, he hid it well. From what I'd seen, he only had eyes for his witch, and the slow perusal he did over my nude body, along with the tundra of his anger, cooled the demon-sized ache between my legs. "Your job is to hunt Fallen and bring them to the Institute."

Why did everyone feel the need to remind me of that? "I've already checked several off the list. The demonologist was a freak, and he's not Fallen. He was some weird mix of magics that Michael and Lilith concocted. Your brother is in league with her, I'm sure of it." I glanced around, noticing a new guardian skulking around the gates. Many entities were associated with the Underworld, especially Hell, but I didn't recognize this one. He was a grotesque beast with a hunched back, horns, and a goat-like beard. He ogled me as he paced, his beady eyes zeroed in on my double Ds.

I gave him a rude gesture. "Can we possibly discuss this after I have clothes on?"

Lucifer blinked, and I was suddenly clothed in the goat's attire. Although he was six inches taller than me, and both of my feet should have fit in one of his giant boots, the material and leather instantly remade itself, so it fit perfectly. I screwed up my nose at the odor, though.

The guardian squawked. "Hey! Those are mine!"

I was no happier about it than he was, although the soft lining of his leather jacket was toasty warm against my skin, and the leather pants fit like a glove. Still, yuck. "This isn't exactly what I had in mind," I said.

The guardian called me a series of vulgar names, and a muscle in Lucifer's jaw ticked. In the next breath, the beast went up in a ball of flame, and I sucked in a sharp breath, the acrid air burning my throat. While I never forgot that Lucifer was an all-powerful being here, there were times when I let myself get casual about who he was and what he could do.

Pressing my lips together and holding my nose against the stink, I cast my gaze to the ground in front of his feet, bowing my head. I was a valuable resource for him, but I was replaceable, and we both knew it.

"I'm looking into the demonologist," he said without emotion, "but the real one *was* a Fallen. Is it possible the version you encountered was him, only he was infected by Lilith's magic?"

Possible, but that didn't feel right. "It's an avenue to explore. Perhaps his vessel was used to create a golem in his likeness that she and Michael filled with their opposing magics."

He was silent for a long time, only the distant screams of tortured souls echoing around us. I waited, remaining quiet and meek—as much as I could pull off—until he ordered me to look at him. "We both know you're not docile, so cut the act." The impatience in his voice was tempered with exhaustion. "You need to get back to work."

Cautiously, I lifted my gaze to his. "Of course. You'll investigate the mole, right?"

He shook his head. "There is no mole."

"How can you be sure? What other answer do you have?"

The king of Hell didn't like being questioned, and it wasn't his best day, but he indulged me. "Until a few months ago, I could not sense the Fallen. After Amy and I found the Lost City of Angels, I knew the rest had to be walking the Earth, but detecting them was a challenge. All that changed when my daughter was born." He paused as if waiting for me to put the puzzle pieces together. When I didn't catch on, he continued. "Since her arrival, I can tap into the Earth's grid and perceive their presence. It's like looking at a map; their angelic energy gives off a pulse."

"That's how you came up with the list."

He nodded and waited again, expecting me to get the gist of what he was *not* saying.

Was this a test? Couldn't he just come out and explain it to me?

I was about to ask him to do so, owning up to my

inability to understand, when everything fell into place. "Michael has the same list."

A nod. "He can tap into the Earth and find them the same way I can."

"Once he became Azaria's guardian, he figured it out. Her power allows both of you to sense where and who they are."

"You understand now?"

I rubbed my forehead. This was not good news. I didn't look forward to hunting down a hundred thousand Fallen, knowing that Michael had probably already gotten to them and left me more surprises. "Our method of finding them and bringing them in isn't working. We need to reverse engineer how we're doing this."

His impatience shifted to curiosity. He'd probably been thinking the same thing but couldn't see a way to improve the process. "How?"

"It could take me years to cover the entire planet and convince them individually to undergo rehab to fight your war. We need something to bring them to us."

He studied me for a moment, his mind working. "Suggestions?"

The seed of the idea had struck in the chapel when I saw the angels gathered and Salmad leading them in song and prayer. "We need an event that will appeal to them on their divine level, regardless of who or what they are now. Something big, like the halftime show of the Super Bowl."

"I doubt a sporting event will attract many of them."

"Not a sporting event. A worship service."

"Only thirty-three percent of those on the list attend church or even believe in God. They don't know who they are, Kali. Even if they have an inkling that God betrayed them. They feel no fidelity to him."

"That makes two of us, or, I guess, a whole lot of us." As the idea grew in my mind, I felt more excited about my new job than I had so far. "They may not worship him, and they may not particularly like you since you and Amy are the ones that got them tossed from Heaven in the first place, but I think there's another being who's tapped into them. One who will be irresistible to them once they feel the call of her request."

He was faster on the uptake than I was. Barely a heartbeat passed before his eyes widened. "You can't be serious."

"No harm will come to her. We only need Azaria to be the beacon that pulls them in."

"Her mother will never allow it. I won't allow it."

Dammit. It was the best idea I had and the most efficient. "Then you'll lose." Saying it out loud was a risk. I would probably be a pile of ashes before this conversation was over. "Michael will win. Sending a foot soldier to recruit your Fallen, convince them of who they are, and get them to the various Institutes in each major country to rehabilitate them is a long game. It will take time you don't have. Michael has only tested the waters at this point. He's toying with you, playing one of his stupid games, and if you don't step up, he'll destroy all of them before your daughter can say 'daddy.'"

We squared off in a stare-down that made me worry again about my continued existence. The only reason he let me live was written on his face when he finally nodded. He knew I was right. "What do you need me to do?"

Phew. No pile of ash today. "Let me put together a strategy, and I'll report back as soon as everything is worked out. I want nothing but top-notch, experienced players on this team. We take no chances, and we hit quick and hard."

"Whatever it takes."

I liked his way of thinking. "I won't let you down."

A blast of heat hit me from the gates, while at the same time, his icy demeanor slapped me in the face. "If you do, it won't be Michael you must worry about. I'll destroy you and everyone you love."

It was said with no emotion, his voice laced with steel. My snarky side wanted to snap off a salute, but the sensible side bent a knee and bowed my head. "I'm at your service."

He snorted. "Get up, and go get some decent clothes on."

Before I could regain my feet, I was on my knees in my bedroom at the Institute. Rad was pacing, yelling into his phone at someone about finding me, his naked body tense.

"Call off your search party," I said, standing.

He looked at me in shock, then screwed up his nose as he sniffed the air. "What are you wearing?"

I waved him off, heading for the bathroom and a hot shower. "Tell Damon to round up the *vitiums*, Cole, Tabriss, and Aphrodite. Have them meet us in the conference room in ten."

I showered quickly, scrubbing every inch of my body. The stink of the dearly departed goat beast was, well, a beast to remove. It was good to get back into my own clothes.

Rad waited for me, now dressed. He came to attention when I swaggered out of the bathroom. I had bagged the clothes but could still smell them. Probably, the insides of my nose were forever scorched with the reek. I held the bag away from me as I walked it to the door. "I've got to burn these, and then I'll be there."

"Neve is bringing food and beverages," he informed me. "Whatever you're planning, I want in."

I patted his cheek. "Of course you do."

He grabbed my wrist before I could exit and pulled me to him. "I'm serious. I know that look in your eye, and you're not leaving me out of this, whatever *this* is."

"I wouldn't dream of it. Now let go of my arm and meet me in the conference room."

He slid his hand to the back of my head and pulled me closer, his lips finding mine. The kiss was long and deep, and I realized he'd been scared when I disappeared on him. The thought warmed my heart, cementing the idea that he truly did love me. I slid my free hand behind his neck, mirroring his gesture as I explored his mouth with my tongue. I bit his bottom lip and flashed him a grin. "And we're not done with what we were doing earlier. You owe me another orgasm."

His eyes flashed with wicked desire. "Damn right, I do."

11

*B*y the time I made it to the conference room, most of the others were already there. Those that weren't would have to catch up with the rest of us later. I didn't have time to wait. "Lucifer and I have come up with a new plan for gathering the Fallen."

Damon had reserved the seat at the head of the table for me, and I considered taking it. It would show my authority to the others, and although I wasn't concerned about Cole, Aphrodite, or even Damon himself questioning it, I knew the other *vitiums*, as well as the head angel, would.

However, I had too much adrenaline flowing to sit still, so I didn't. I paced, working through ideas in my head at the same time. "Hunting them one by one isn't working. We need to bring them to us using the natural connection they feel toward each other and to their savior."

Salmad sat forward with his usual solemn frown, interlacing his fingers on the table. After our last altercation, I knew he'd be against all my ideas. "God cast them out of

Heaven. They feel disconnected from Him, as well as his Son. How exactly do you plan to restore that?"

"Not God or Jesus. Azaria. She's their savior."

The attendees glanced at each other, confused. All except Damon. "You want to use her like a magnet to attract them."

I touched the end of my nose, letting him know he was on the right track. "Lucifer can locate them, thanks to Azaria's connection to them. That's how he came up with the list. I believe we can use her to contact each of them and draw them to a central location."

"The Institute isn't big enough to hold that many," Cole said. "We certainly don't have enough room to train all of them."

I lingered at the end of the table, placing my hands on the chair's high back. "Right, you are. Even if this trick works and we get most of them to search for her, our resources are limited. With the Institutes all over the globe, we have options, but it will still be overwhelming for most. That's why we have to do this in waves. First, I want to see if it works with a small local group. If it does, we scale up, using the already trained Fallen." I pointed at Tabriss. "I want you to create at least three teams to command operating bases in the tri-state area. Think of them like military posts. We'll make sure each one is secure and supplied with everything you need. Avoid highly populated areas in case there are any...*accidents* with their powers."

Di raised her hand. "How exactly are you using Azaria to draw them in?"

I was still working on that, but I had a strategy. "They need to see her, so I will have JR create a short video we can send each of them. It will also contain instructions on where we want them to travel to. That's why we have to get the bases set up first."

Rad toyed with one of his guitar picks, flipping it end over end between his fingers. A restless habit. "Some of the Fallen live on the streets without access to technology. Some of them are drug addicts and mental patients. Even more are behind bars for crimes they've committed. How are we going to reach them?"

"They'll be the second or third wave once we work out the kinks. For the initial wave, you, me, and Cole will handle them."

The War demon and the Chaos demon traded a glance. Half the time, they wanted to kill each other; the other half, they watched football games and talked about expensive cars like the best of bros.

Tabriss made a face, obviously a bit put out. "The Fallen in residence here are still rehabilitating. You can't ask them to go out in the field and—"

I cut her off. "All boots on the ground. We don't have time to baby you and yours. Get Josiah to help us find the rest of your friends. If you have a better idea, I'm listening."

Everyone's attention turned to her, and her cheeks flushed. Josiah was her second in command, and I wished he was their leader. He was so much easier to handle. "All I'm saying is that you're asking a lot from us."

Neve burst in at that moment with a tray of pastries, a carafe of coffee, and insulated paper cups. She wheeled her chair to the reserved open spot, and Di jumped up to help her unload her haul from her lap.

At that point, I lost control of the meeting while everyone

grabbed brownies, cookies, and turnovers and poured themselves coffee.

I snagged a brown sugar scone that was still warm. It melted on my tongue and tasted like Heaven. Once I'd downed half of that, I grabbed coffee, still turning ideas over in my head.

"Okay, everyone back to their seats," I called over the din of voices. "We need to look at this idea from all angles and pick it apart. When we initiate it, I want as few problems as possible."

We spent the next hour strategizing and troubleshooting. Damon was exceptionally quiet, but the others had plenty of things to say, most of them annoying to me. I tried to channel him, rather than my inner bitch, and listen to their concerns, as well as their suggestions. Then, I began doling out assignments. "Damon, I need you to find us three locations in the tri-state area. Tabriss, you and Josiah select your teams and assign responsibilities. Aphrodite can help you prioritize the rehabilitation sequence, but you'll need someone responsible for meals, sleeping arrangements, and training."

"And what exactly are you doing?" she snipped.

I downed the last of my coffee and crushed the cup in my hand. "I'm in charge of global networking and getting the video." As Lucifer had warned, Amy would be as reluctant about using their daughter for this. "If anyone has any questions or problems, direct them to me."

Damon stared at his cup. "If anyone has questions or problems, *I'll* handle them."

Okay, then. "For now, is everyone clear on what you're doing?"

Salmad cleared his throat. "Who is going to see to everyone's spirituality?"

"You and the rest of the *vitiums.*"

Our squad glanced between him and me, none of them saying a word. Unusual, to be sure, but I was grateful they weren't arguing.

On the other hand... Tabriss stood, squaring off with me. "What about Michael? You said he's already gotten to some of the Fallen before you did. What if he finds out about our plan?"

It was one of the reasons I'd hesitated about including her in this meeting, but I never had only one plan. Even if I'd left her out, she'd learn about it all in due time.

Plan B—her obsessive connection to the archangel was too good to pass up.

I smiled at her, and even though it probably looked more like a grimace since I couldn't stand her, at least my voice came out friendly. "Michael knows every name on the list because he is Azaria's guardian. He's tapped into her abilities, not her mind. He'll only know about this plan if someone in this room tells him."

The insinuation hung in the air like dust motes laced with acid. She set her hands on her hips. "You think I'd tell him."

It was a statement, not a question. "I think your love for him keeps you hovering on the edge of a thin line. I strongly suggest that you remember how he walked away from you in my cemetery because you'd ingested demon blood. My blood. He no longer cares about you, Tabriss. You don't owe him loyalty or love."

That shut her up. She stomped from the room, leaving the door open in her wake.

"What do you want me to do?" Rad asked.

There were a multitude of things I wanted him to do, but a few had to wait. My smile turned genuine. "You and Cole will come with me to Sweet Investigations to talk to JR and—"

Before I could finish, my body stiffened, an icicle of angel magic shooting down my spine. The hand holding the crumpled coffee cup began to fade.

"Not again," Rad said, leaping to his feet.

I swore under my breath. "Not now, Lucifer! I'm in the middle of a..." I choked, the ice hitting my throat and closing it up.

In the next moment, I was once again transported through time and space, but the place I ended up in wasn't Hell.

"There you are," Michael said with a delighted grin. He was eating grapes, chewing each one slowly as he looked me up and down from a golden throne. "My favorite little demon. We need to talk."

12

*A*t least I wasn't naked.

The environment was bleak, with a watery azure light coating the horizon. Sand blew across the tops of my boots, and monoliths of ice jetted from the uneven ground around us.

It was neither hot nor cold, but the invisible magic hanging in the air was heavy with an electrical charge. The tips of my hair lifted off my shoulders, and the tiny ones on my arms stood at attention.

The ice left my throat, replaced by a coating of dust. It filled my nose, making it itch. "Pretty sure we don't have anything to discuss, angel boy."

His grin grew as he chewed another grape. Out of the watery air, a puppy appeared in his lap.

Not any puppy—Milena.

She appeared content, staring up at him with her big eyes while she wagged her tail. He glanced at her, stroking her fur. "Do you like being Lucifer's bitch? Isn't that what humans call it in prison when you have to bend over and take it?"

I sure as hell didn't like it, but I had no choice.

I started to be flippant about the situation not being a prison, but wasn't it? If I didn't do what Lucifer wanted, he could wipe me and all those I loved out of existence.

I tried not to show any concern for the dog, even though I wanted to snatch her out of his lap. "Don't you have someone to feed you those?" I pointed at the fruit. "Wasn't that Tabriss' job? She misses you, you know. It was a dick move to walk away from her."

The grin fell off his face, and his wings fluttered. The throne had slits in it for them.

The puppy jumped from his lap. I had to give her points for that.

"Although you can't stage a rebellion against my brother and stop hunting the Fallen completely," he said, "you must allow me to sabotage your efforts."

Right to business, then. "Why would I do that?"

"If you don't, and the prophecy comes true, what do you think will happen to your kind?"

Sparring with Michael was never fun, even though I prided myself on my superior skill—both with words and with weapons. I paced to the nearest ice outcropping, where the dog sniffed at the base. "You've never worried about demons before. Why do you care? Why wouldn't you want to see Heaven and Earth reunited?"

"I have my reasons. What I don't understand is why you would help Lucifer bring about your own demise. I thought you were smarter than that."

The puppy barked, and I caught movement inside the ice. Was there something in there? I peered closer, instinct causing me to press a hand against the cold surface. The sand around the foundation kicked up, swirling in a counter-clockwise direction. The frozen block trembled under my touch, and whatever was inside shifted, a face coming into view. I dropped my hand and took a step back. Was that...a person?

Michael was grinning again, and I wasn't sure if it was due to the jab or the fact he'd shocked me.

"What game are you playing this time?" I snarled.

He finished the last grape, tossing the stripped section of vine over his shoulder. It landed in the sand and was immediately sucked under, disappearing from the surface. "If anyone is going to reunite Heaven and Earth, it will be yours truly, not Lucifer's brat."

He wanted the glory. Duh. Why hadn't I seen that coming?

I studied the ice sculpture again, mainly to act like I was thinking his proposition over. A second glance showed me the face was familiar—a balding head, wire-framed glasses, and a weak chin. *Merde.* "This is the demonologist. The real one. You've trapped him here." *Whatever here is.*

He tapped his temple with a finger. "You're catching on, but you're failing at the snappy comebacks. I expect more from you." He crossed his legs and eased deeper into his seat. "Honestly, I was looking forward to this, but you're definitely not up to your normal speed."

"I'm lacking decent material."

He grinned. "That's more like it." He waggled his fingers at me. "What else you got, *vitium*?"

Coming from him, the label sounded like a curse. I ignored the challenge and surveyed the other monoliths, searching my brain for a way to save the damn dog if this went sideways. *When* this went sideways because it would. For the moment, I needed a distraction. "Are these all Fallen?"

"A collection of the most powerful." He surveyed the landscape, much like an artist surveying his latest painting. " You could say I've put them on ice." He smiled at his joke. "Now, who needs to work on his material?"

He ambled down the steps. Why did he seem so much taller here than when I'd met him on Earth? Did Earth cause him to shrink?

Towering over me, his wings flared big and bright, and he lifted the tiny dog, holding her up in one hand to look her in the eyes. She whined, and I tensed. "I'm about to offer you a deal I have never offered another being in my eternal life." He lowered the puppy, tucking her into the crook of his massive arm. "I would advise you to consider your answer carefully and do yourself a favor—accept it."

"And if I don't?" I forced my unease over the dog's vulnerability aside. "Let me guess, you'll harm those I love. Been there, survived that, and we made a deal that you'd leave them alone."

"This old dog"—he made air quotes with his free hand and pointed at himself—"has learned a new trick."

I waited for him to go on, but the ghost of the smile on his lips suggested he was again using irony and expected me to acknowledge it.

I glanced at Milena and back at him. "Okay, *old dog*. Do I have to give you a treat for you to perform?"

The smile grew. "Better, and yes, I expect a reward in the end."

As if we were bargaining, he waited for me to agree. "This isn't my first angel joyride. You have an eternity to play these games; I'm on a deadline. Let's get to the part where you threaten me, and I tell you to fuck off."

His eyes lit. "No threats. Not this time. I've learned motivation is often better doled out as a reward, a treat. Aren't you listening?"

Was he dangling a carrot? I steeled myself not to look at the puppy. Did he believe I was attached to the animal enough to do what he wanted, just to get her back? "I'm all ears."

"I have something you want. Help me sabotage Lucifer, and I'll give it to you—plain and simple."

"Lucifer already promised to give me my family. Afraid you can't top that."

This took him by surprise. "Has he now? Hmm. That's generous of him, but since he knows I was going to give you control over Hell, it's not much of a reward, is it? That's the reason you wanted to be in charge, right? To be reunited with your parents and sister?"

Where was he going with this? "You were never going to allow me to control Hell."

"Oh, ye of such little faith." He clucked. "If Lucifer wins, there won't be any Hell. You know this. I know this. And since you're a *vitium*, you'll end up stuck with the rest of us in the new Paradise, but your family will cease to exist. Your demon and Undead friends, too."

I kept my fear of that off my face. "Living with you in Paradise is its own kind of Hell for me. No offense."

He laughed, enjoying the verbal sparring now. "I feel the same about you, my dear demon."

"So you want to offer me a better deal?"

"The deal is that we defeat Lucifer together. You're already part of his inner circle, and he's entrusted you with saving his Fallen brethren. All you have to do is let me get to most of them first." He waved a hand around the area. "Ice them. If you can't find them, you can't save them. No new Paradise, and you'll still have a chance to rescue your parents and sister."

"Lucifer will figure it out." The ongoing fight between these archangels wore on me. "Here's a thought—why don't you man up and face your brother? Use those big angel balls, get in his face, and throw a few punches. Beat each other black and blue, and call it a day."

"Demons." He tsked and shook his head. "You think you can solve everything with violence."

"Not everything, but we've been using the four F's, just like humans, since the beginning of time. Both humans and demons have flourished, so while the peace lovers look down their noses at us, it works."

"The four F's?"

"Of survival." For all of his modernism, he was still dense when it came to many, many things. "Fighting, fucking, feeding, and fleeing. Fleeing as a last resort or when the odds are overwhelming. Live to see another day and all that."

"The war between Lucifer and myself is ancient. It cannot be resolved with a simple punch to the face."

"You might be surprised."

He studied me as though reevaluating his prior belief that I was intelligent. "Here's the deal." He set the puppy on the ground and withdrew a small bound volume from his robes. "I have something you want, something to help you with the end of days."

My breath caught—I recognized what he held in his hand. "Is that...?"

He fanned it in the air. "I see I've got your attention now."

A Catholic priest had once told me there were three Books of Revelation, all prophecies transcribed by my father, John of Patmos, from my mother's visions. She'd been an oracle.

The first one was found in part in the King James Version of the Bible, but the second, which described the necessary measures to stop the Whore of Babylon and the Beast, and a third, which revealed the whereabouts of a divine army who would assist those on Earth to stop the apocalypse, had been hidden in the papal chapel in Rome.

I'd retrieved one of them on a trip there, but Lilith had tossed it into a fire, destroying it.

Now, lost in this freakish desert, I knew I was staring at the same opus. My mouth went as dry as the sand-whipped air. "How? Lilith..."

The dog mosied over to sniff at the demonologist again. I felt a tremor ripple beneath my feet. Maddy, my young vampire friend, watched any and all movies, and she'd recently been on a Tremors binge. Dune, too. All I could think about when I felt the ground shake and saw the sand shifting was that some giant worm was about to break free and devour me.

"I'm an archangel," Michael said with a *duh* tone. "Don't you think I can recreate a simple text?"

It was so much more than simple. Did he know the contents? "Why would you?"

"This is the treat." He shook it in the air like a preacher with a Bible, chastising his congregation. I wasn't sure if he intended to strike me with it or wanted me to subjugate myself to it. "You want your daddy's book, and I want you to help me."

We already knew about the divine Fallen army. My mother had predicted they would help stop the apocalypse. Now, they might bring one—but only for those of us who were not redeemable. "Is that why you teamed up with Lilith?" I asked, taking a long shot. "Some warped partnership to use magic to resurrect the text she destroyed?"

"I don't need the mother of demons in order to use magic. I broke you out of that warded Institute and brought you here, didn't I? Replacing a book is child's play."

How *had* he removed me from the Institute? I'd have to figure that out later.

I held out a hand. "Let me see it."

"Don't trust me?"

"Why would I?"

He tossed it at my feet. The puppy ran over, curious, and nuzzled it. Seemed too easy, and while I was anxious to flip the pages and view my father's writing, I smelled a trap. A trick.

I nudged the dog away with my toes. "Doesn't matter, does it? This book is about the Fallen, and we already know about them. It's more of a keepsake for me, seeing as how my father transcribed it from my mother's visions, but in this war, it doesn't help us."

He narrowed his eyes, wings rippling with irritation. "What do you want, then?"

"There's nothing you can give me that Lucifer can't, and you can't win the war without your sword. Buttering me up and asking me to turn traitor isn't going to work."

"You demons are all alike," he snapped.

"Actually, we're not. There are many levels of us, and some aren't that evil. Just like there are different levels of angels, and some of you are lacking in the divine department."

"How about this?" He held out one of his giant hands, and a coiled leather whip appeared in it. "What would you do to get your beloved weapon back?"

My heart did a funny jig inside my chest, and I found myself reaching for Volante before I even thought twice. The handle snapped to attention and quivered as though she felt my presence and was as happy as a loyal dog to see me.

He snatched her away before I could grab her. "Not so fast. I've offered you two things of great value to you in exchange for your word that you'll help me. These are things you cannot get any other way, regardless of what you think Lucifer is willing to do for you. What do you say? Do we have a deal or not?"

Michael was as attached to his sword as I was to my whip, yet he hadn't asked for it. Why?

It was true what I'd said—not all angels were good, and not all demons were bad. Every part about this smelled like a trap, but I couldn't figure out what he was up to.

I had nothing to lose by asking for more. "I want the demonologist."

If my request surprised him, he didn't show it. In fact, his wings settled. He thought he'd won. "I assume you have a good reason to want him?"

I had to think fast. "Nope. I want a show of faith. I appreciate the book and the weapon, but like I said, neither has any bearing on the war. I'll have to keep them hidden, or Lucifer will be suspicious. So, I need to plant someone inside the Institute who won't draw suspicion but who can keep tabs on my boss and the Fallen already training there. Someone who can fit in and will only report to me."

He crossed his arms and pinched his chin between his finger and thumb. "How can you be sure he'll be loyal to you?"

The dog sat at my feet, leaning against my leg. She looked up at me with her puppy eyes, and I tried to ignore the way they tugged at my heart. "You let me worry about that."

"I want to know your plan."

I smirked. "Don't trust me?"

He chuckled. "Not at all."

"Good. Then we understand each other." I decided to go balls to the wall, knowing he was caving and I'd better take advantage of it. "There's one more thing."

"Why am I not surprised?"

"Come on. You have to admit you're getting off easy."

He wiggled his fingers in the air again. "What else?"

"A slice of Paradise."

"Come again?"

"You heard me. I don't care which of you wins the war, but I want a free pass for myself, and those I decide are worth saving."

"You want to save the other *vitiums*."

Them and a few more. "My family, too."

This must have satisfied him. He nodded. "It's done."

I doubted that. In my book, Michael had done a lot of good in the world, but he wasn't an ally and certainly didn't care about what happened to me or the rest of the demon population now or down the road. He would personally wipe all of us out of existence if he could.

Which made me think about his flaming sword again.

He tossed Volante to me, and I caught her, hugging her to my chest. Then I cried out as a sharp pain cut my palm. I looked down to see myself bleeding. The blood dripped into the sand and was absorbed by it. The dog sniffed the air, coming to all fours. "What was that for?" I demanded.

"Our bargain is sealed in blood," he said, and I saw a few drops falling from his hand as he squeezed it into a fist. They, too, were absorbed by the sand, and another of those tremors rocked the ground under my feet. "You are now bound to me, Kali."

The ice monolith encasing the demonologist cracked in half, the pieces shattering as they fell.

The Fallen blinked at me from behind his spectacles and waved his arms wildly. "You need to get out of here. You can't trust him!"

Michael chuckled. "You can both leave now," he said.

He snapped his fingers, and I went cartwheeling through time and space, landing on my ass in my room at the Institute. The dog and the demonologist appeared, too.

"What have you done?" the man shouted at me.

I got to my feet, stroking my whip. "Saved your ass. A little gratitude would be nice."

"Don't you know better than to make deals with angels?"

"Don't you know better than to make deals with Lilith?"

He stared at me in shock. "How did you know?"

"I know a lot of things."

"Then you should know you can't beat Michael."

That's what the archangel thought, too.

Boy, was he going to be in for a surprise.

13

I stormed out of the room, the demonologist yelling behind me.

"Where are you going?" he called, running to catch up. The dog trailed last in our congo line. With no time for the elevator, I raced for the stairs.

"Where are we?" His voice fell farther behind. "You can't leave me here. She'll—"

The stairwell door slammed shut, cutting him off.

By the time the dog and I burst into Damon's office, I was breathing hard. A packed crowd greeted us. Damon sat at his large mahogany desk surrounded by Cole, Rad, Yasmine, Kirill, the *vitiums*, Tabriss, Di, and Neve. Last but not least was Dru. Who'd called him?

Total relief flooded Rad's face. He pushed through the group to embrace me. "There you are."

I wanted to take a second to enjoy that embrace, but there wasn't time. "Hold that thought."

"Milena!" Di cheered. "You found her!"

The dog rushed to her. She scooped it up. "Where have you been?" Her voice took on the tone one used with a baby. "There's Mama's good little girl."

"You were worried about the dog and not me?" I asked.

A slim, ringed hand waved me off. "You can take care of yourself."

"You shouldn't have named her," I remarked. "Damon won't let you keep her."

"Milly isn't going anywhere," she said in that baby-talk voice. She rubbed the dog under the chin. "Are you? You're my little sweetheart."

The demonologist lumbered into the room, panting. All eyes went to him, and he stumbled back a foot. "What in Heaven and Hell...?"

I yelled over the rumble of voices that broke out. "Listen." I slid past the others to get to Damon. "It was Michael who snatched me, which means he can access this place."

Damon's brow furrowed. "That's not possible." His gaze snagged on Volante. "How did you get your whip back?"

"Long story, not important. If Michael has a connection to something—or someone—already inside here, he can access all of us."

The crowd fell silent. For a heartbeat, Damon didn't so much as breathe. Then he shot to his feet. "Tabriss."

While I wanted a reason to toss her out on her angelic ass, I shook my head. "She's been here for months; he only tried it today. The artifacts—remember the way she reacted to them? How she said she could sense him?"

"The pouch nullifies their magic."

"Not when they're close to Michael's sword," the demonologist said between gasps. "But you don't have that, so..."

"Who is that?" Damon scowled.

"Frankel Bahar, demonologist," I said. I motioned to Damon. "Frank, this is Damon, archdemon and head of the Institute."

Frank blinked behind his glasses. "For real?"

Damon didn't oblige to reply. "This is the Frankenstein monster you told me about?"

His tone suggested he was unimpressed. "No, this is the real Bahar," I told him. "The one Cole and I encountered was a fake."

"Who created the fake?" Kirill asked.

Frank adjusted his glasses, his breathing resuming a normal cadence. "Michael and Lilith."

A cacophony of questions erupted, and I had to whistle to shut everyone up. "We'll get back to that in a minute. Right now, we've got to get those artifacts out of here."

Damon was already in motion. "All of you—out! Now." He didn't often use his archdemon voice, and its power reverberated through the air, propelling all of us toward the door like a gust of wind. "Except you," he said to me.

My limbs locked in place. I shot Cole a *help me* look.

He sneered and patted my shoulder on his way by. "Good luck."

Damn. Frank was the only one left with me when the door closed.

"You need my help," he said when we both glared at him in question. "And this...whatever it is...is partially my fault."

"Because you raised Lilith," I accused.

He made a head gesture that was neither a yes nor a no. "I was attempting to summon Michael, but I think my resource was tampered with—the ritual was...off."

Damon motioned for him to turn around. He did, and Damon went to the safe. "Summon him for what?"

"The text I was translating had odd forms of angelic symbols. I wanted him to explain them to me."

"You don't mess around, do you?" I asked. Nabbing an archangel was dangerous. "Why him?"

Damon removed the pouch and dropped it like he'd been zapped. He swore in Spanish and shook out his hand. "Something jabbed me."

I grabbed his hand and examined a puncture wound in the center of his palm. Black blood welled there. "That can't be good."

Frank hustled over. "What's in the container? The artifacts you mentioned?"

I reached for my sword, but it was MIA. I had to use the toe of my boot to flip over the pouch instead. The sharp end of the brooch's pin had pierced the side and was covered with Damon's blood. "Better have Kirill treat that," I said, a sick feeling in my gut.

"You've been pricked by a prick," Frank muttered with a touch of humor. "Don't mess around with it. I can see the glow of Michael's essence. Angel mojo is nasty stuff, especially for your kind."

Pricked by a prick—I couldn't have said it better myself. "You can see a glow?"

He glanced at me, his thick lenses making his eyes appear bug-like. "Can't you?"

I shook my head. "I can feel it." Grabbing Damon's landline, I buzzed Kirill. He didn't answer. I pushed several buttons to engage the building-wide PA system. "Kirill, Damon's office. Now."

"Stat," Frank said.

I hung up the phone. "What?"

"He's a doctor, right? In hospitals, they say, 'stat.'"

Hiding my eye roll, I muscled my boss into his chair against his will. From inside his bottom desk drawer, I pulled out a blade he hid there in case of unexpected visitors.

"What are you doing?" he asked.

"Not touching the pouch," I answered and stabbed the thing with the end of the knife. "Wrap your hand."

He grabbed a few crumpled napkins from the waste can to staunch the blood.

With the pouch dangling on the blade, I held it out in front of me, moving for the safe's open door. It was dark inside. "What about the sword?"

Damon rose from his chair and withdrew a velvet bag from the interior roughly the length of the blade with his good hand. "It's still here."

Frank slid closer. "Can I see it?"

This time, my response was in unison with my boss's. "No," we both said.

His shoulders slumped. "Does it truly burn with a blue flame? I don't see any glow."

And I didn't feel Michael's magic coming from it. "Verify it's real," I said to Damon.

He handed it to me with the bag still on. "It likes you better."

"The big, bad archdemon doesn't like angel steel?" I teased.

He glared. "If it's booby-trapped, I'd rather not die today."

Oh. "In other words, I'm expendable."

He rolled a finger in a *get on with it* motion. "I don't want it to taste my blood. That's the only reason."

It was a good one, but I doubted it was the only one.

I dropped the pouch into the waste can and scooted it to the door with my foot. I would handle it in a minute.

Carefully, I undid the drawstrings of the bag, the velvet caressing my skin. The blade quivered, and I stopped, letting my magic slip inside and touch it.

It leaped three inches into the air, and I was so startled I barely caught it when it fell. "What was that about?" I groused, even though I didn't expect either of them to answer.

"Seems happy to see you," Frank said. "Why do you guys have Michael's sword, and how did you get it?"

"Later. Right now, I want to ensure it's still here, and then I have to get those artifacts out of the building."

No more messing around or taking it slowly. I reached in, grabbed the hilt, and...

I was knocked on my ass when the blade launched itself at me.

I landed on the floor and slid. My head whacked the door just as Kirill swung it open without knocking.

Like a dog who hadn't seen its master in days, the sword attacked, but not in a vicious manner.

Because it wasn't Michael's.

It was the one Cole had given me.

It sank against my chest and purred, rubbing its hilt between my breasts.

"Why are you on the floor?" Kirill peered down at me. "And this better be good—I don't take orders from you, Kali."

I managed to stop the sword's molestation and got to my feet with it in hand. "It's for Damon, you jackass."

He glanced at the desk. "What's wrong with... Oh."

Damon had passed out in his chair.

14

*L*eaving Damon with Kirill was hard, but I had to trust that our resident medical expert could handle the infection, even if it came from an angel. Seeing my boss knocked on his butt and unconscious made my gut cramp and my hackles rise. If Michael had done anything to him...

What will you do? I asked myself. Not only was Michael an archangel, but he also had his sword again, giving him the ultimate power over all of us. What exactly did I think I could do to him? Kill him?

Laughable. I'd scored a couple of hits since I'd known him, but the bottom line was that he could squash me like a bug.

Why hadn't he?

Frank tagged along as I made my way to the underground parking garage. On the way, we encountered Cole. He fell into step with me. "Where are we going, and why are you carrying a wastebasket?"

"Michael has his sword. I need to get the artifacts out of here immediately."

"That's what they were for?" At my nod, he swore and grabbed a set of keys off the pegboard. "He's coming?" He jabbed a thumb at Frank.

"I can be instrumental," Frank assured him.

Cole looked at me and rolled his eyes. "Whatever."

As we climbed into one of the Land Rovers, Rad appeared in the doorway. His face was furious, but his eyes were hurt. "No goodbye? You just take off?"

"It's an emergency." I adjusted the sword, feeling annoyed and guilty simultaneously. Why did it seem like I was constantly apologizing to him?

Cole slid out of the driver's seat and threw the keys to him. "You drive, Guitar Boy."

"That's more like it!" He sauntered to the SUV, giving me a pointed look.

Cole went to the back and opened the hatch, pawing through an assortment of weapons under the floorboard and coming out with a shotgun. He grabbed several boxes of ammunition made with various metals and a few with hollow points filled with silver and holy water. He tossed the boxes into the backseat. They smacked into Frank, and he flinched, scooting as far from Cole as he could when the War demon climbed in with his new toy.

"Rad should stay here," I argued.

"Suck it up, buttercup." Cole slammed two cartridges into the open barrels and closed them with a sharp click. As Rad stuck the keys in the ignition, Cole slapped the back of his seat. "Let's go."

We peeled out of the garage, tires squealing. "Where to?" Rad asked.

I closed my eyes against the setting sun as we exited the parking lot and hit the street. "I don't know yet. Just drive." Traffic was light. I took a deep breath, reaching out to Lucifer. *We need to talk.*

Telepathy wasn't my strong suit, and I had no idea if the king of Hell was paying attention to me or the Institute, but it wasn't like I could call him on the phone. When there was no response, I added a more earnest appeal. *This is important. It can't wait.*

I toyed with the ring on my necklace, wishing it worked both ways—to transport me to the Institute and Hell if need be. Or take me wherever Lucifer was at the moment. My own little version of Lucifer GPS.

There was still no response. Cole and Rad were waiting for more information.

Rad eyed Cole in the rearview. "Since when don't I have to fight you to drive?"

They were both alphas—territorial and consistently trying to outdo each other. Always intent on proving who was stronger, faster, and more dominant. "He's anticipating an ambush," I said before Cole could respond. "He wants to be prepared, and driving takes too much of his focus."

"Ambush?" Rad glanced around, surveying the road, other drivers, and buildings. "Why would you leave the Institute if you think someone will attack you?"

I pointed at the contents of the can. "The artifacts created a back door for Michael to grab his sword. We had to get them out of there because—"

"Angels are assholes," Cole supplied. "This whole thing

is bullshit. Helping Lucifer raise an angel army? Taking on Michael? Working with either one of them in order to unite Heaven and Earth? In doing so, we eliminate ourselves. What the fuck are we doing, Kali?"

He said 'we,' but the underlying connotation was 'you.'

What was I doing? I wasn't sure anymore. Seemed like I'd become such a pawn of the Institute's, of Damon's, I was going against my natural, demonic essence.

Frank spoke up. "How exactly does Lucifer intend to do such a thing?"

"With you—his Fallen army," I told him.

"Ah. That's why Michael kidnapped me and the others."

"Yep." But I was starting to think that was less about sabotaging Lucifer and more about doing so to me.

With Michael, everything was personal.

"You really think Lucifer stands a chance against him?" Rad asked.

I wasn't sure about that, either. "I don't even know why he wants to return to Heaven."

"Well, it's not like we're great to hang around with," Cole said. When I flicked my gaze to him over my shoulder, he added, "Present company excluded."

I rubbed my forehead, leaning back against the seat. "Lucifer isn't answering me."

"What do you want to do?" Rad asked.

"We need a safe place for those artifacts," Frank insisted.

"Yeah," Rad said. "The Institute *was* that place."

I couldn't call Lucifer on my phone, but I could call his witch. "We need Hell."

Rad slid his gaze to me. "You want me to drive to Hell?"

"Oh, no," Frank said.

I searched my call log for the number I needed. "I want Lucifer to take them off our hands and secure them there, but he's off-grid."

"I can summon him," Frank offered.

I swiveled, Rad snorted, and Cole ground his teeth together so hard I heard the enamel shearing off. "You don't *summon* Lucifer," I told the demonologist, "Trust me."

Frank shrugged, miffed. "Fine. I was only trying to help."

"*Can* you summon him?" Cole asked. He saw my shock and shrugged. "What? Might be a good tool to add to our arsenal."

Frank lost the peevishness and puffed up his chest. "I've trapped high-level demons and low-level angels with no problem."

"Like Lilith?" I asked.

He deflated and had the good sense to be contrite. "I told you I was attempting to summon Michael, but the incantation and ritual had been tampered with. I ended up with her instead."

Had the ritual been wrong, or were the two of them working together as I'd suspected? "You're sure Michael didn't send her in his place?"

Frank thought about that for a whole two seconds. "Not possible. It's very specific to the demon or angel you're trying to call."

"Except you got Lilith rather than Michael. Your logic doesn't hold water."

He harrumphed, pushing up his glasses. "You don't understand. It's all in the sigils and the Language—language with a capital L."

"I'm familiar with Enochian."

"This is something else." He waved it off as if I were too dumb to get it. "It's a phraseology style unlike any written language."

I held up my phone. "Let's try calling Lucifer's girlfriend first."

It rang on the other end three times before Amy answered. "I already said no."

"Sorry, what?"

Her air magic hummed through the connection. I had the urge to disconnect in case she would hex me somehow. "I won't have my daughter turned into a social media icon."

Lucifer must have told her my idea. "The only people who will see the video are the Fallen. I give you my word."

If it had been any other angel reincarnate, they probably would have laughed. She didn't because she knew I had protected her and Lucifer several times, most notably from Lilith and Michael over the past year. "I get what you're trying to do, but you need to understand..."

"I would feel the same way," I interrupted, "but I've looked at this from every angle, and the only way we can raise your army quickly is by putting out a call to them. Even though she's a baby, she has power beyond anything this world has ever seen. You and Lucifer should be with her when we do it. I think the three of you together will have the most impact. Those Fallen who have no clue who they are or why they're here won't be able to resist any more than the ones actively searching for answers."

The line was quiet for a long moment. Rad continued driving, staying off the interstate but avoiding downtown as well.

"Please think about it," I asked her. "In the meantime, I

need to speak to Lucifer. It's important, and it can't wait. I tried reaching out to him mentally but got no reply."

She gave a humorless chuckle. "No surprise there. He's with Azaria right now. He's really struggling with something. I'm not sure what it is—he won't discuss it with me. Do you know?"

Let's see... Locating and rehabilitating a hundred thousand Fallen angels? Using his daughter as a promotional piece to draw them in? Fighting with his big brother Michael? "He's always brooding. Are you sure this isn't him being him?"

"This is more intense."

I watched the passing scenery, scanning the darkening sky for any sign of an angel with a sword. The artifacts seemed to pulse inside the waste can, like beacons sending him our whereabouts. "I have no idea, and I wouldn't bother him unless it were an emergency. Tell him I have a new theory to replace the previous inside mole one."

"I'm sure I don't want to know what that's about." She sighed. "I'll let him know, but no promises."

She hung up.

"Well?" Rad asked.

"Now we wait," I said.

And pray my new boss doesn't hang me out to dry.

*A*fter an hour, we stopped for gas. I considered offloading the artifacts in the dumpster behind the station, but with my luck, some innocent human would find them and start Armageddon.

After that, we went through a drive-through and loaded up on burgers, fries, and shakes. Food in hand, I sent Rad west to the apartment Lucifer had provided me, and I had yet to see.

For most of the way, everyone was silent. I connected my phone to the Land Rover's Bluetooth and played my favorite heavy metal playlist. Frank complained; I ignored him. Music always helped me think.

As the miles passed, the traffic leaving Chicago grew thinner. The darkness of open fields soothed me, broken up here and there by headlights traveling in the opposite direction.

Because of our driver's lead foot, we made it to the apartment in an hour. It was in a decent part of a small town, but nothing fancy. The population was less than any of the Chicago burbs. Lawns were mowed, and their main street was lit by solar lights that were decorated with old-world flair. The shops were a mix of empty storefronts and small businesses.

The apartment complex itself was plain and nondescript, with a weedy parking lot behind the building that it shared with a small convenience store next door.

Never trust the devil. It was something Damon had once said to me. As I stood looking at the entrance to the apartment building, it flitted through my head again. "Where's Zayfeer?" I muttered.

"Who?" Rad asked.

The others joined us on the sidewalk, Cole watching our backs. "Lucifer's bitch."

Rad frowned, still confused. I tapped the side of the waste can. "He was watching us with an eagle eye when we were on the hunt for the Fallen, but now he's nowhere to be seen. Amy mentioned Lucifer is more sullen than usual."

Rad shrugged. "And?"

I hauled out my phone and hit redial.

Amy answered on the first ring. "I gave him the message," she said. "He left."

"Any idea where he went?"

"I thought to see you. He didn't show up?"

"Where's your angel nanny?"

"I have no idea."

Crap. "Is there anywhere Zayfeer would go to hide from Lucifer?"

She paused. "Why would he need to hide?"

This was all my fault. I didn't like the angel, but I didn't want Lucifer to snuff him out because he thought Zayfeer was the mole. "Think, Amy. Where would Zayfeer go?"

"I'm right here, demon." The angel in question appeared on the lawn, dressed in a biker outfit. He eyed me with suspicion. "Thought you'd get me fired, did you?"

"Never mind," I told Amy. "I found him."

"Luc?"

"Zayfeer."

"Is Luc with him?"

"No." I switched subjects. "Do you believe Michael will protect Azaria, even if she's the key to reuniting you and Lucifer with Heaven and creating a new paradise on Earth?"

Her pause was heavy and laced with a combination of annoyance and suspicion. "Do you know something I don't? Is he going to hurt my daughter?"

A couple strolled down the sidewalk. When they saw our group, especially Zayfeer, they turned around and hurried away.

Amy trusted Lucifer with everything. She and their daughter were the only leverage I had. While I didn't like scaring her for no good reason, I couldn't honestly reassure her that her daughter was safe with Michael. "Do what you have to do to protect her. I'll get back to you."

I cut off her questions and pocketed the phone. "Where is Lucifer?" I asked Zayfeer.

"He's in a meeting."

"With...?"

"None of your business." A cop car crept down the street, its headlights throwing weak illumination toward us. "I suggest we take this upstairs."

"Who is that?" Frank murmured to me as we headed for the building. "I don't recall any angel named Zayfeer."

"I'll catch you up later." Behind the angel's back, I gave Cole a sign we used for ambush when in the field. He nodded, his massive self disappearing around the side of the building instead of following us inside.

Rad watched all this and silently slipped a blade out of his jacket. Frank sensed danger and slowed to stay behind me.

We trudged up the stairs in silence and Zayfeer didn't seem to notice we were one person short when he stopped outside the apartment door. Placing my hand on the frame, I sent magic into the room to check for enemies or traps.

Zayfeer gave me an aggrieved eye roll as if I were the stupidest demon ever to walk the earth.

The energy that zapped me made me drop my hand and take a giant step back. "What the...?" I faced him. "You said he was in a meeting."

"Yeah, with you, idiot. Stop keeping him waiting."

But it wasn't only Lucifer's energy I sensed beyond the door. It was similar, but more like Michael's—aggressive, forceful, dynamic. Like a pitbull on a leash looking for a fight.

I didn't bother lowering my voice because I knew they could hear me even if I did. "Who's in there with him?"

Zayfeer slouched against the wall and brushed at nonexistent dust on his shiny black jacket. "Open up and find out."

I glanced at Rad and Frank, swallowed, and braced myself. Using my magic, I opened the door, ready to haul ass in case I was about to be attacked.

Lucifer and another angel sat at a small kitchen table,

completely overwhelming the two tiny wooden chairs on either side. They peered at me and then at each other with a knowing glance.

While Lucifer was dark and dangerous, the other angel favored Michael—blond hair, blue aura, and androgynous features. He wore a bland-colored shirt and khakis that looked straight from The Gap's last closeout sale. "That's her?" he asked.

Lucifer nodded.

The newcomer surveyed me again. "*She* took on Michael and tricked him into giving her his sword?" He laughed as if that were the most humorous thing he'd heard in a while. "Our brother must be losing his touch."

The demon in me scratched at her cage, becoming the pit bull on a leash. "Who the Hell are you?"

Frank peaked around me. "Uh oh. Is that who I think it is?"

Cole came stomping up the steps. The gun was ready to fire. "Move."

I stopped him with a hand and motioned the three of them to stay put. I didn't care what Zayfeer did. Then I put on my *don't mess with this demon* bitch face and swaggered inside.

"Michael isn't losing his touch." I thunked the waist can on the table between them. "His sabotage scheme with these artifacts was nothing but a ruse and a distraction. He now possesses his sword, and Damon's infected with his angel essence."

Lucifer kicked back, unconcerned. "We know," he said.

I blinked. "You know?"

Zayfeer strolled to the tiny kitchen to help himself to a

drink from the refrigerator. "I figured it out while you were off doing"—he glanced at Rad and Cole filling the doorway —"whatever."

Rad marched to my side while Cole hung back, gun still poised to fire. I covertly motioned for him to lower it. He ignored me.

Facing the two angels again, I scanned the rest of the apartment that I could see. Nothing set off my magical warning system, but it was already on high alert because Lucifer was so close. He was the most perfect, most beautiful being I'd ever laid eyes on, and my vice and virtue warred with each other over how to react every time I came into contact with him. My demon alternated between hiding and throwing herself at her prison bars, wanting to bow at his feet.

Clearing my throat, I stepped back from his immense sexuality and power. "Who are you?" I asked the other angel.

He flicked his eyes to Lucifer again, seeming surprised and disappointed. "You didn't tell her?"

Lucifer ran a hand over his face. Like before, he looked tired. Worn out. A young child could do that to you.

So could a brother who wanted you dead. "Kali, this is my brother Thelesis. The, this is Kali Sweet."

"Thelesis!" Frank rushed to my other side. "You mean Archangel Raguel?" He held out a hand. "It's so nice to meet you. I'm Frank Bahar."

Lucifer quirked a brow. I shrugged. "Meet your newest Fallen," I told him and patted Frank on the back. He looked like he might pee himself, fangirling over the newcomer. "Frank, in case you missed it, this is Lucifer Morningstar."

The smile fell from his face. His body locked up like he'd been stunned with a taser. "Lucifer... You... He..."

His eyes rolled up in his head, and he fainted.

"Why do you have that effect on my friends?" I asked and saw the corner of Lucifer's mouth quirk in what for him was a smile. I glanced at his brother. "One of the other *vitiums* did the same thing when he saw him at the Vatican, and the timing couldn't have been worse." Salmad and I had been escaping the Pope's private quarters, and the only way down was to jump to the courtyard from a high balcony. Half of Rome had been watching, and the Swiss Guard, along with a bunch of Noctifacters, had been closing in. I'd had to pick Sal up and jump off that balcony with his dead weight over my shoulder.

Thelesis stood, rising to his full height, and I planted my feet. He'd been acting calm and friendly. Now, the pit bull returned. "I've heard a lot about you, demon."

"You have me at a disadvantage. I don't know you." Rad's Chaos magic made the ends of my hair rise. "So which is it," I asked. "Thelesis or Raguel?"

"This," Lucifer said, eyeing his brother, "is your angelic counterpart."

My trip through the tunnels under Rome to sneak into Vatican City came rushing back. It was the first time I'd learned about him. "The angel of vengeance." The words came out breathy. I smacked myself before I started doing a Frank-at-a-Swift-concert impression. "But..."—I ricocheted between him and Lucifer—"It's not a good idea for us to be in the same place simultaneously. Amy told me it would cause a karma-something-or-other. An unbalancing."

Thelesis smiled with dark delight. "And I believe you

once suggested I was...what was it? Ah yes, 'chickenshit' to meet you. Wasn't that how you put it?"

Only mentally. "You read my mind?"

He stretched out his arms and his power grated against my skin. "Angel, here, *duh*. You may call me Thelesis." Glancing at this audience, he made a satisfied face. "No karma-clysmic event, but there is an unbalancing effect if we're together too long, so let's make this quick. As you may remember, I'm the sheriff in this realm, keeping Fallen and demons in check. At times, I must step outside my given jurisdiction"—he gestured at those of us gathered—"and rein in an archangel. Michael is out of hand."

"Which is why you stole his sword and gave it to Amy," I said, "to aid us in stopping the Horsemen."

"And now, thanks to you, he has it back. He's creating an unbalance between Heaven and Earth yet again."

"He's raising his own army," Lucifer added. "He can't raise a hand against my daughter, but he *can* wage war on the Fallen."

Michael was no kind, loving soul, that was for sure. If all of us banded against him... "What happens to the prophecy if he succeeds in destroying the Fallen?" I asked. "Can you still be united with Heaven?"

"The idea is to bring everyone back into the fold," Thelesis explained in a tone suggesting I had the IQ of a snail. "Not only Lucifer but all those who left. That is the point."

I tried to swallow my sarcasm. It didn't work. "Is it? I thought the point was getting rid of sin and allowing humans to live in paradise."

He waved one giant hand through the air, brushing that away. "That's a result of reuniting the angelic kingdom."

Now, we were getting to the truth. "So all of this has been a smokescreen. You don't care what happens to humans—it's all about the angels."

The brothers exchanged another of their subtle, cunning glances. Thelesis gave me a wormy smile. Behind it, I saw him considering several responses. "Lucifer said you love humans. How unusual for a demon. Then again, without them, who would you have to torment?"

I looked at the king of Hell's expression. His steady gaze didn't waver a bit. "Why is Thelesis really here?" I asked him.

He pushed to standing. "Kali, meet your new partner in our battle against my brother."

The pit bull held out a hand, his smile turning cold and vicious. "It's time we raised a little Hell, don't you think, demon?"

16

*W*ith that slick smile still in place, he glided toward me. I had a split-second vision again —this one of him putting an arm around me.

I backpedaled, determined not to let him touch me. I ran into a wall of Rad and Cole. They radiated a menace that I felt right through my clothes. "No offense," I growled at Thelesis, "but I can raise hell on my own. Tell me your plan, and let's get on with it."

Thelesis stopped his approach. The smile melted off his face. "Fine." His snippy tone suggested I was a party pooper. He snapped his fingers, and two more entities joined the party.

Two more who also made my skin crawl. I stared at the female whose face showed nothing of her thousand-year-old existence. Instead, she appeared twenty at most, whip-thin and dewy-eyed. "Moira?" I whispered.

She took in the gathering with a quick once-over. "Her?"

she said to Thelesis. "You never said I'd have to work with a vengeance demon."

Frank chose that moment to stagger to his feet, chattering about demons and archangels. We all ignored him.

"Who is she?" Rad murmured in my right ear.

"It's Faron," the Fate answered for me. She was the personification of destiny, all tied up in a hundred-pound package. "I don't go by Moira, Atropos, or any of those outdated names anymore."

"And you?" Cole demanded of her male counterpart.

From the look of him—tall, broad-shouldered, and muscle-bound—he was Cole's twin. His odd energy tasted bitter on my tongue. His eyes, sizing up Rad, were the silver of glittering smoke and vowed death to all who crossed him.

Wasn't this going to be fun?

"That's Bane," Thelesis volunteered. "Since part of my divine purpose is ensuring harmony, and things have not been harmonious for a good long time, I've called in an expert to help us out."

Things hadn't gone well for me the last time I'd encountered the Fate. I wasn't excited about this development. "How exactly?"

Faron withdrew a lollipop from her back pocket, unwrapped it, and stuck it in her mouth. Tossing the wrapper on the coffee table, she plopped down on the sofa, crossed her legs, and then popped it out of her mouth with a loud noise. "My sisters have other talents, but mine is *eventuality*. Everyone has to answer to me eventually, whether by death or consequences." She took another pull on the candy. "Even angels. The thing is, fate is not one single outcome written in stone, like everyone believes. I offer your team guidance regarding which outcome is most likely to occur, depending on the circumstances you create with your actions."

It sounded recited, as if she'd given the same speech a thousand times.

Maybe she had.

Lucifer crossed his arms, impatient. He summed it up for me. "There are six Fallen who will give us a better chance against Michael if we get to them before he does."

"Faron can tell us which ones," I added, clarifying this new plan.

"Eventually, harmony must be restored," he said. "With Thelesis and Faron joining our quest, we have a leg up on Michael."

Bane and Cole were locked in a staredown. Rad's chaos energy was circling them both. In all honesty, the demon in me wanted to see the three of them in the ring. I still wasn't sure *what* Faron's partner was, but it wasn't anything I'd encountered in my three hundred years.

Since she was considered outside the realm of gods, angels, and a host of other divine beings, I suspected he was, too. If she could serve up fate to any being in the universe, what—who—was to keep her in check?

Bane?

His steely gaze slid to mine as if he heard my thoughts. With a confidence I didn't feel, I gave him a smile. His top lip curled, and he dismissed me with a lazy scan before returning his attention to my bodyguards. Interesting that he found Cole and Rad the most dangerous threats in the room.

I made a mental note to fix that.

"Who are these chosen six?" I asked.

Thelesis pointed at Faron. "She has the list and will get you started."

Hauling herself up, she gave a disgusted sigh. "Let's get this over with."

"I don't work well with others," I said, holding Lucifer's gaze. "We've had this discussion."

Zayfeer chuckled. "All I know is I'm glad to be rid of her."

"Stop complaining," Lucifer barked, and the room vibrated with power. I wasn't sure if he was speaking to his nanny or me. "We find the six and restore Paradise. Then you can be on your merry way."

Several things about his statement made me pause, but one idea had been bugging me now for days. "Humans call on Michael for protection and guidance. If you succeed, they'll no longer need either, right?"

"Correct," he bit out. "They'll no longer pray to my brother for help. What of it?"

Not only would they no longer need Michael, they wouldn't need God. There would be no Hell, no sin. They wouldn't need a savior, commandments, or freedom from oppression.

No wonder Michael wanted to stop this. Who would he be without their adulation and obsession?

Bane wasn't the only one who could read my mind. I saw Lucifer tense, the lightbulb flashing over his head like a strobe light. "No wonder he's so determined to stop you," I uttered. "Here, I thought he was just pissing in your sandbox, but in reality, he'll cease to exist if Paradise is restored. Humans won't need him or you."

Faron found that amusing. "That *is* one possibility," she

said with a wink. "It's that *be careful what you wish for* outcome."

Thelesis whipped his head to look at Lucifer. Even he hadn't considered that hazard. "Are you confident you want to continue down this path, brother?"

"It's what's best for humanity," I insisted. All turned their attention to me as if my statement were heresy. I didn't back down. "Isn't it supposed to be about them?"

Faron rolled her eyes. "I see you haven't changed a bit. Still rooting for the underdog."

Our encounter a hundred years ago had been over the fate of a human-demon hybrid. A being who'd had no say in their heritage but was being used as a pawn by both sides of their family to try and destroy the other. Caught in the middle, the fourteen-year-old female had come into her demonic powers when puberty kicked in. She'd been provoked into horrible outbursts after being kept in a dank basement, beaten, and starved until the abuse had woken her evil side.

The Bridge Council had sent me to investigate after we received an anonymous call about her, but I'd been too late to save her and exact the justice she deserved. Her demonic father sent her to wipe out her human mother's side of the family when she was in one of her rage fits. She was captured by human police and ended up committing suicide while in a psych ward for young offenders. The night she decided to take her own life, I met Faron outside the girl's locked door. I was determined to break her out of the institution and take her to the Council, where she would learn how to control her powers and understand it wasn't her fault.

Faron had prevented my intervention. I still carried the guilt on my conscience.

"I value many things," I snarled at her, "including the underdogs of this world. What I don't value is the idea that free will only works up to a point. Fate, destiny, prophecies... those are tricks of the mind. False beliefs that power mongers like you and Michael force down our throats to make us compliant and weak."

Bane bristled. His lip curled again, and he reached for a steel blade that could gut any living thing in seconds. His touch caused it to glow. "Watch it," he growled.

Cole and Rad matched his fury and became bookends on each side of me. "She's right," Rad said. "You're all playing games and using us as pawns to get your way." His chaos wind kicked up and slammed into the Fate and her lapdog, knocking them off their feet. Good thing the sofa was there to catch them. "Don't forget who you're messing with."

Zayfeer set down his glass. "That's my cue to leave." He winked out.

Bane bounded to his feet, pulling his blade, but Faron was equally fast, grasping his arm to stop him. Her eyes went milky white for a second before they flicked back to their usual turquoise. "Fighting amongst ourselves won't end well."

Guess she would know.

Rad allowed the wind to die. Frank backed toward the exit, plastering himself against the door. "I'll just wait downstairs."

"No," Lucifer said. There was no menace, but the angelic mojo rippling off him made my bones tremble. I swear, I saw the outline of his black wings. "Your skills are needed."

"I shall take my leave now, though," Thelesis said. His wings rippled with a shudder. "Time for Kali and I to go our separate ways." Like Zayfeer, he disappeared.

"Divide and conquer?" I asked, hoping I wouldn't have to work with the Fate and her bulldog. "They can search for three, and Cole and I will search for the others."

"I'm going with you," Rad insisted.

Lucifer looked like he wanted to be anywhere but stuck in the apartment with us. "We don't know where they are."

I did a double-take. "What do you mean? You have the list."

"I have been unable to determine their whereabouts. They are not on Earth nor in the Lost City."

Nothing was ever easy. "But they exist, right? Are they in some kind of purgatory? Did they end up in Hell? Can't you just use your angel GPS to find them?"

The suggestion he might not know the six Fallen were in Hell earned me a searing glare. "They exist, and we will find them."

"How?"

Yep, he was pissed—the outline of those black, glossy wings became sharper. The boss didn't like being questioned.

The Fate interceded. "Seven angels held high esteem in Heaven but left their powers to follow Lucifer. As with all Fallen, they've received a bad wrap on earth, thanks to Christianity."

The number seven was continually cropping up. "Are you referencing the seven principles and powers?" I asked.

"Been studying your Bible?" Faron asked.

Thanks to Salmad, more than I cared to. "Why are we only looking for six?"

Lucifer glanced at Frank. "You've already found one."

If Frank could have melted into the floor, he would have. His gaze bounced around between all of us, finally landing on me and sticking. "I don't know what you're talking about. I'm a demonologist. That's all."

"We haven't had the full talk yet," I explained to Lucifer. I gave Frank a weak smile, trying to force some sincerity into it. "You're Fallen, Frank. One of the original angels who gave God the finger and rebelled against Heaven. I brought you to the Institute so you can learn about them and how to help yourself and Lucifer with the coming war."

His nervous laugh filled the room. "Right. Good one."

When none of us laughed with him, he cut off abruptly and widened his eyes in shock. "You've got to be kidding."

I turned back to Lucifer and Faron. "I know where the other six are."

"Where?" Lucifer demanded.

He wasn't going to like this. I hated what I was about to suggest too, but it was the only way for us to rescue them. "Michael has them imprisoned in a desert where he's king. That's where I found Frank."

Why had he agreed to give me this one of the crucial seven that Lucifer needed to sway the outcome in his favor? Did he not realize their importance to the war? Was it some kind of trick?

"How do we get to them?" Rad asked. "And don't say that you're going to make a deal with that asswipe."

"She already did," Frank said. He pointed a finger. "She's bloodbound to Michael!"

Always the hard way.

Lucifer bore down on me, and it was all I could do not to cower. "You betrayed me?"

My insides went fiery. "Wasn't my idea! But you need a double agent to uncover what he's up to." I swallowed the hot agony rising in my throat. He was going to fry me from the inside out. "I *am* bloodbound to him, which gives you an advantage." I fell to my knees at his feet, my joints turning liquid.

"Stop it," Rad threatened, reaching for my arm. His chaos scent of the wild ocean filled my nostrils. The sofa lamp careened into the wall, shattering the base. The salt and pepper shakers on the table smacked Lucifer in the back of the head with enough force to rock him.

Rad went flying, slamming into the wall so hard that the room shook. Hell, the building felt it.

Lucifer lifted me off the floor, my feet dangling. Cole stepped in front of Rad's prone body. He knew he could do nothing for me; protecting Rad was what I wanted.

"Michael has your principalities..." I force-whispered through the neck vise Lucifer held me in. "I can free them."

"Not if I exterminate you," he growled.

My body burst into flames.

eeing yourself as a living torch is one of the seven wonders of the world.

Not.

This must be what Hell feels like. I wasn't melting on the outside, yet my organs, blood, and bones boiled on the inside.

I would have screamed, except for the fact that my vocal cords blazed with a violent inferno, and Lucifer continued to squeeze my neck into a pulp.

My demon roared in my chest, blasting her magic at Lucifer.

He didn't even flinch.

"Wait!" Faron's voice was a background screech.

Hers wasn't the only one—Cole and Rad were also shouting. Since neither ran to me or attacked Lucifer, I assumed he had them pinned to the wall.

Through the blaze of agony, I saw my tormentor flick his gaze to the Fate. "What?"

Faron moved into my peripheral vision, her eyes milky again. "Perhaps... Yes. She's telling the truth. She intends to doublecross your brother, not you. She's your strongest ally." Her head tilted as if she were viewing a movie behind her white orbs. "She's your only hope."

The vise released, the fiery torment instantly gone. My body dropped to the floor at Lucifer's feet. I coughed and choked, sucking in cool air. My skin felt as if I had a bad sunburn.

"Get up," he ordered.

Blinking away my double vision, I rose on trembling legs. "I would never..." It came out a croak. I had to clear my throat several times, my vocal cords raw. "Betray...you."

He rocked back on his heels, his arms crossed, seeming to consider this declaration. I stood as still as possible, but my body shook with what felt like an earthquake's after-shock from his assault. I kept my eyes cast downward, playing the subservient little demon he wanted—but I couldn't have raised them even if I'd wanted to.

Was Faron's prediction accurate? Was my bold statement?

I've been alive too long to say I would never do some-thing. Circumstances and situations had forced me to perform services I disliked and commit to alliances I hated.

The room was quiet and still, everyone waiting for Lucifer's next move. His intense regard made me twitchy, and I found it difficult not to fidget. Sweat ran along my hair-line and trickled down the back of my neck under my collar.

I'd survived plenty of torture in my day, but never anything like that. Comparing it to the time he'd given me the plague, I rated this attack worse. With either, he could extend the agony out as long as he wanted to, and a tiny part of me felt sorry for those in Hell who suffered his torment over and over.

"Look at me."

A rush of soothing ice slid into my limbs. The trembling eased. I lifted my gaze.

The expression on his face reminded me of my father's when I'd disobeyed him. "Tell me exactly what happened between you and Michael."

I did, describing the desert, Michael's throne, and the ice prisons. I mentioned my father's book, the fact that Michael had returned my whip, and his promise of a slice of Paradise for those I cared about.

At the mention of that, Lucifer's attention flipped to Cole and Rad. Behind his hateful glare, something softened—he was thinking of Amy and his daughter.

On some level, we were the same—we would do anything to save those we loved.

He huffed an angry breath. "You're a shrewd negotiator."

As hot as the inferno he'd created inside me had been, the icy sensation swept through me, refreshing. I sighed with relief, my demon quieting. Lucifer's magic caressed her like a cat.

Shocked that she would allow it, I nevertheless was grateful for her cooperation. "The bloodbond wasn't my idea," I told him. "He exacted it against my will before I knew what was happening."

"That's true," Frank said.

I glowered at him over my shoulder, noting that he'd sought shelter in the corner. He glanced away, refusing to meet my eyes.

Traitor.

As suspected, my bodyguards were imprisoned behind an invisible wall. They pounded at it and yelled, but the wall was soundproof, cutting off their protests.

Making eye contact with each, I offered a reassuring smile and a wink to let them know I was okay. Still angry and looking like they wanted to rip Lucifer apart limb by limb, they at least stopped their attempts at breaking free.

Facing Lucifer again, I bowed my head slightly. "I convinced your brother to give me Frank so I could use him as an insider at the Institute. This will allow me to feed Michael information, although I will have to do a few things to make him believe that I'm sabotaging your attempts to fulfill the prophecy."

His eyes narrowed. "Such as?"

"I could use a few hours, maybe overnight, to devise a plan. We need a way for me to free the six without Michael suspecting that's my goal. There's nothing I can offer him as a trade since he must already understand their importance to your success. I can't even hint that I want them, or he'll suspect a double cross. Is there any way you could sneak Frank and me into his desert kingdom? We could free them and return here before he even knows it."

Lucifer shook his head. "He'll be prepared for that. Now that he has his sword, he'll most likely use it on them."

The fact that I hadn't thought of that made my stomach twist. All of this might be for nothing.

Frank shuffled up from behind me. "He can't use the sword against another angel, not even a Fallen."

"Not true," I told him. "When this whole thing started, he gave me the sword to use on Lucifer." I motioned at my boss. "As you can see, I didn't do that, but I did send a Fallen, who I put in Lucifer's place, to the great beyond with it."

Frank looked stumped. "That's not supposed to be possible." He paced away, rubbing his chin and shaking his head. "But he won't kill the six if they're so important to the war's outcome." He turned to face us, his eyes brightening as he raised a finger. "That's it. That's why he was working with her."

"What are you talking about?" Lucifer asked.

"Lilith." Frank returned to my side, nodding his head adamantly. "They made a bargain, and that must be what he promised her—that she could have us in exchange for her help."

"Help to do what?" I asked. "What does an archangel need the mother of demons to do for him?"

The brightness on Frank's face evaporated. He glanced at Lucifer and back to me, eyes wide with something to fear. "Oh, boy. Or maybe I should say, girl."

"What?" I wanted to shake him. "Tell us."

He swallowed hard. He couldn't quite seem to meet the archangel's eyes as he stammered and shifted his weight from foot to foot. "Michael may not be able to harm your daughter because your wife asked for his protection for her, but..."

Understanding hit like a ton of bricks. I gasped and looked at Lucifer. He met my eyes with the same fiery, angry inferno that had burned inside me only moments before.

Faron put a hand to her mouth, and even though she wasn't seeing the future, she got it, too.

Without hesitation, Lucifer freed Cole and Rad from their prison. The two clamored toward me, grabbing me and checking me over to ensure I was truly okay. I batted away their fussing hands, my stomach bottoming out. "You need to go," I said to Lucifer. "Check on Amy."

His full lips were a thin line of wrath. "We're all going," he snarled, and the next thing I knew, I was hurling through time and space.

18

*W*e landed in Amy's ice cream shop, a milky, sweet fragrance mixed with an underlying scent of bleach.

The archangel Gabriel was scooping multiple types of ice cream into a bowl and barely paid us any attention as we crashed into several tables and chairs. He quirked a brow at Lucifer, who pointed upstairs and took off running.

A silent message conveyed, Gabriel dropped the scoop, narrowed his eyes at us, and took off after him.

Two customers in a booth jumped up and fled out the door, causing the bell to jingle hard enough that it fell off.

I disengaged a metal napkin holder from my spine and caught my breath, staring at the ceiling. I was running low on everything—sleep, food, and patience. Too much angel magic made me irascible, and if Lilith was here—if she had hurt that little girl...

Rad's face appeared above me. I accepted his extended

hand, and he pulled me to my feet. "We are in a mess of shit," he muttered. "Are you all right?"

I straightened my shirt. "I now know what it feels like to burn in hellfire, literally, but I'm fine."

Frank was rubbing the back of his head as he sat up, having clocked the corner of one of the tables. Faron and Bane stood off to the side, arguing in strained whispers.

Cole was already checking the windows and searching for any sign of Lilith. "Should we follow them?" he asked, gesturing in the direction Lucifer and Gabriel had disappeared.

I shook my head. "We fan out around the perimeter and see if we can pick up any evidence she's already here."

"And if she is?" Rad asked.

"We'll have a fight on our hands." I longed for one of Amy's espresso milkshakes. My limbs felt heavy, and my brain numb. I jerked Frank to his feet. "Any chance you can sense your fellow Fallen?"

His hair was matted on one side, his glasses askew. Dark shadows had formed under his eyes, and he shook his head, looking as bad as I felt. He massaged his lower back. "This quantum jumping around takes it out of you, doesn't it?"

"Better get used to it." I disliked the creepy, crawly sensation inching over my skin. "Can you tap into your angel mojo?"

He straightened his glasses, then removed them, staring through them before he cleaned the lenses with the edge of his shirt. "I didn't even know I was an angel until a few hours ago. I don't know what it's supposed to feel like."

"Never mind." I rubbed my forehead. A headache was

taking shape behind my eyes. "I can't smell her or any hell-hounds. Can you?" I asked Rad.

He shook his head, confirming that my Lilith radar wasn't screwed up. "Nothing. Did you really make a deal with Michael?"

"Like I told him"—I pointed toward the second floor—"I had no choice. He hijacked me into it. We can use it to our advantage, though."

In his blue-eyed gaze, I could see that he wanted to crush me in a hug simply to reassure himself that I was alive and functioning. He did me the favor of not creating a public display. "I hope you know what you're doing."

Cole started barking commands, ever the War demon ready for a fight. "Bane, you're with me. We'll cover the rear. Rad, you and Kali stay here and guard the front. Frank, you and Faron search the interior, top to bottom, and be sure Lilith hasn't left behind any surprises."

"Surprises?" Frank squeaked.

"Bombs, bugs, traps," he rattled off. "A sleeping hell-hound, ready to wake at her command. The usual."

Faron and Bane stopped arguing, and the bodyguard took two steps toward Cole. "Who put you in charge?"

I positioned myself in front of him. "I did. I don't know what you are, but Lucifer put *me* in charge of handling the rescue of his Fallen. I've tangled with Michael more than once and survived. Lilith, too. Oh, and The Four Horsemen of the Apocalypse. Cole has been with me through all of it and understands the battlefield better than any of us. You can either join Team Kali or leave. Your choice."

He snarled like a wolf and started to respond, but Faron interceded. "As his name suggests, he's a nightmare to work with," she said. "Misfortune, torment, you name it, he's the one to carry it out."

Something flickered behind his gaze so fast when it cut to her that I almost missed it. Affection? Whatever these two had going on between them reminded me of myself and, well, just about every male I knew. While I could handle any extreme situation, they all tried to protect me and sometimes save me from myself.

"I can see where you could be an asset to us," I said. It was true. Faron could see the future and outcomes based on our decisions. Bane could carry out some of those less palpable decisions. "But understand this. There is a hierarchy here. Your opinion will be respected, but you'll report to Cole and, ultimately, to me. You'll have to leave if you can't handle that." I flicked a subtle look at her before returning to him. "And FYI, if Lucifer brought Faron here, he won't let her go with you should you choose to leave."

He growled menacingly again, not so much at me but at the situation.

"We're wasting time." Cole realigned our jobs, leaving Bane out of the picture. "Rad and I will cover the back. Frank can stay with Kali, and Faron can look for boobytraps."

Bane fingered his blade, but his tight posture softened when Faron laid a hand on his arm. "You are my cross to bear," he murmured to her.

She brightened as if that statement made her day. She punched him in the bicep, grinning. "You love every minute of it."

I clapped my hands softly. "Great. Team Kali it is. Let's get on with this."

A witch in a bright yellow and pink dress ran into the room from the back. "Gabriel?"

She pulled up short when she saw us. Her hands flew up, instantly making a sigil in front of her in the air with her ringed fingers.

Before the spell could knock us on our asses, I touched my index fingers and thumbs together, creating a bubble shield. It formed barely in time to bounce the magic back at her.

Her reflexes were quick. She ducked behind the ice cream counter and shot another spell at the fan above me. The thing disconnected from its down rod, spinning as it fell.

Frank yelped. Faron ducked. Rad and Bane leaped. Rad knocked me sideways as Bane grabbed one of the blades and frisbeed the whole thing across the room at the ice cream freezer.

Glass shattered. The witch jumped up from her hiding place, glass in her kinky, dark hair. "Oh, now you're in trouble," she said, fire in her eyes.

Her scent was smoke and spice, ashes and needles. A Vodun priestess. This was Amy's best friend, Keisha.

I held up placating hands. "We're here with Lucifer. We mean you no harm. There's a threat against Amy. He's upstairs with Gabriel, checking on her and the baby."

Her already narrowed eyes squinted tighter. "You should've led with that. You're the vengeance demon, Kali Sweet."

I nodded. "You didn't give me a chance to explain."

She brushed at her shirt, eyeing the destroyed ice cream freezer and shaking out her kinks. Shards of glass hit the floor. "We're a little jumpy around here these days." Her attention went upward. "Are they okay?"

No shouts, screams, or fireballs yet. "I believe so. You haven't caught wind of Lilith around here, have you?"

Her dark brows scrunched. "No. She better not come after us, either, or I'll…" She drew herself up, fingers in motion. Another sigil formed, but this was of protection. When it flared to life in the air in front of her, my magic wiggled. "I better fix this before Amy sees it," she said, staring at the busted freezer.

Cole motioned at Bane, and they walked out. I jerked my chin toward the back, gesturing for Frank and Faron to get started looking for any traps. Rad shadowed me as I stepped toward Keisha, glass crunching under my boots. "Want help?" I asked.

She glanced at said boots "I have a pair just like that. They don't have the spikes on the side, though. I can see where those might come in handy." She waved a hand, and the fan, embedded in the wall, screeched as it pulled free. A heartbeat later, it was back in its place in the ceiling. I wasn't sure how she reconnected the wires, but the blades began to spin again. "I can't take a chance with the ice cream. We have to get all new tubs."

That was the least of our worries, and serving customers might be put on hold. However, allowing her to do something was a good way to keep her calm.

She murmured a few words under her breath, and the shards of glass lying around us reconnected in mid-air, reforming the front and sides of the freezer. More pieces lifted from the five-gallon containers inside, fitting themselves into the display case again.

Footsteps sounded overhead, and she worried her bottom lip with her teeth. "Hurry. Clean up the mess you made, and I'll get these out of here."

She held out her hands over two of the buckets, and they lifted from their places, flying out of the open space at the back of the display. She sent them toward the room from where she'd emerged.

Rad and I righted tables and chairs, keeping an eye on the front door and the activity out on the street. All seemed normal, and since we'd been here previously, we had a good sense of what 'normal' was for Eden.

By the time Amy blew in, Lucifer on her heels, the parlor looked respectable—except for the missing ice cream in the display case.

"Kali," she said, throwing her arms around me in a hug. "What is all this about Lilith? I thought you sent her back to Hell. Is she walking the Earth, thanks to Michael? Who are those people searching my office and storeroom?"

I disentangled from her arms and locked the front door, flipping the sign to the closed side. Keisha elbowed Gabriel and led him out. The two returned with a cart full of new five-gallon buckets.

"It's a long story," I told the air witch. I glanced at Lucifer, who nodded, confirming that we were safe. But his wife needed something to do with the hands she was worrying in front of her. "Would it be possible for me to get one of your delicious milkshakes while I fill you in?"

She glanced between us, and he placed a hand on her shoulder, giving it a squeeze. She twirled a long strand of her brown hair around her finger. "You'll protect her, right?"

I didn't need to ask who she was referring to. "With my life."

"Zayfeer is watching her while she sleeps," Lucifer said. "I've added an extra layer of wards under those already in place."

The shop sat on a portal to Hell. While I could feel the magic that Amy and Keisha had originally sealed it with, Lucifer's additional layer sat metallic-like on my tongue.

Since we didn't know where Lilith was at the moment, there was no harm in taking extra precautions, and since she didn't seem to be already present, we might have preempted whatever she and Michael were planning.

"Michael is sworn to protect Azaria, and even if he has cut a deal with Lilith, he cannot be derelict in his duty," I reminded everyone. "That's not to say he won't find a loophole or that the powers that be won't offer an opportunity."

I thought about Faron and her ability to see different outcomes. From what I knew, the Fates couldn't tell the future until a choice was made in the present, but I'd have to grill her in-depth about that.

If we could formulate different possibilities of what Michael and Lilith could do together, could she tell us which had the most likely chance of harming the girl?

In any case, we had to be ready for all potential outcomes.

Amy turned to watch her friend and Gabriel replacing the tubs. She didn't ask why. She cupped her hands over her face, took a deep breath, and let it whoosh out of her. "You're right. If anyone can beat Michael at his own game, it's all of us." She marched behind the counter and snatched up a tall cup. "One coffee mocha ice cream shake coming up."

My day was already looking up.

19

"We should move Amy and Azaria to the Institute," I told Lucifer around a mouthful of ice cream.

He didn't so much as blink. "No."

We were gathered in Amy's office while Gabriel watched camera feeds of the front and rear exits. Cole and Bane continued their outside perimeter security.

"This place is warded to the nines," Amy said, rocking their sleeping child in her office chair. The girl's white-blond hair curled around her ears. One chubby hand rested on Amy's collarbone, the thumb of the other in her mouth. "There's no safer place."

I jabbed my spoon into the melting treat. I had anticipated resistance, but I was running low on patience. "It sits on top of a Hellmouth. Hell, remember? Where Lilith lives."

No one appreciated my sarcasm except Faron. She idled in the corner, pretending to be engrossed with filing her nails, but I saw one corner of her mouth rise.

"It's been sealed," Keisha stated.

"Seals can be broken," Rad countered. He knew I was right. Lucifer did, too; he just didn't want to admit it. "The Institute is the safest place on earth for you right now," Rad continued. "Between the demons who are well acquainted with Lilith and her strategies and the angels who will go to any lengths to protect you, you already have a trained supernatural army at your disposal."

I spooned more ice cream, savoring the smooth creaminess and caffeine I desperately needed. "It's a well-oiled machine, run by an archdemon who can outthink all of us."

Like a magnet drawn to steel, Amy's gaze went to Lucifer. He stood staring out the single window in the room. His shoulders were tight, the magic radiating off him, making the ground under my feet buzz. Every few minutes, I sent my own energy spiraling downward, checking the perimeter under the building for any sign the seal was weakening. Due to the thick wards, it was a challenge for my demon to draw up her usual amount of magic, and even the caffeine and sugar I was inhaling weren't enough to overcome the weariness in my body. I needed red meat, a long sleep, and a good workout with lots of punishment to replenish her.

I spoke to Lucifer but knew my words would register with Amy. "Lilith won't expect you to take Amy and the child there. She would never risk her own neck to infiltrate the Institute."

"So she'll send someone else," he argued.

"She doesn't have anyone powerful enough, outside of Michael, who could."

Faron, who seemed to be bored with the whole discussion, blew on her nails and pocketed the file. "You definitely can't stay here," she told him. "At the moment, Lilith is making plans to blow us all up."

That got everyone's attention. We came to our feet like an orchestrated dance, and Lucifer whipped around to glare at her. His wings went nuclear, flaring around him, the tips hitting the ceiling. "You're only telling me this now?"

A lesser being would have dropped to the floor and groveled at his feet. "It's not going to happen this minute. Maybe not at all." She flipped a cool glance to me and Amy, who clutched her daughter hard enough to rouse the girl from slumber. Those unemotional eyes slid back to him. "It's simply one of the things she's considering doing, and she's gathering the resources to do it."

He raked a hand over his face. Silent communication passed between him and Amy, and then he gave a sharp nod. He pinned me with his intense eyes, the fires of Hell raging behind the dark irises. "Get them both to the Institute. Use the ring."

"Do I have time to grab a bag?" Amy asked Faron.

The Fate nodded.

Lucifer barked orders to Rad and Keisha. Rad left to round up the others while the Vodun priestess went to help Amy gather what they needed for themselves and the girl.

When everyone was gone, Lucifer, Faron, and I formed a triangle. Lucifer started to say something to me, then stopped himself. Some internal decision made, he gave me a curt nod. "I'll alert Damon that you're coming so he can prepare."

That he would leave Amy in my care spoke volumes. "Or I can go tell him, and you can stay here with your family," I offered, suspicious.

He didn't argue or offer any reason for his plan. He simply blinked out, and it was just Faron and I.

"Can you read my mind?" I asked.

Her eyes skimmed my face. "Possibly. Why?"

"If I think of an action, something I'm going to do but haven't put into play, can you tell me the odds of success based simply on the thought?"

She sauntered to the desk and sat on the edge. "Depends on how much intent is behind the thought. For example, Lilith has a lot of intent and momentum behind her goal of stopping the prophecy. Any plans she makes are easy for me to pick up on, but I can't see the outcomes simultaneously. I can only see the one she is actively pursuing."

"Like bombing this place."

She nodded. "Everyone expects her to use magic to kill the girl, but she's realized that since Azaria is in a physical body, she can postpone the prophecy if she annihilates said body. No magic necessary. All she has to do is create a catastrophic event."

"Lilith not using magic? I didn't see that coming."

"Nor did she. It wasn't her idea."

"Michael?"

"His role is to protect the girl from danger, but only up to an extent. If the bomb is meant for her parents, she'll be collateral damage. His will cannot overrule that of her guardians' choices. Although she is a babe, free will still plays a part in her life, as it does with every life. The actions of those who care for her subject her to various threats and dangers. He cannot interfere with that."

"In that case, she won't be safe at the Institute either, will she? We need an underground bunker."

"Speak to Damon. I believe he has been making plans for such circumstances."

I tossed my cup in the trash can. "You're pretty handy to have around. I'll have more questions for you once we secure the package with him."

She boosted off the desk and gave me a saucy wink. "I knew you would."

I climbed the stairs to the apartment to hurry things along with Amy. Through the door, I heard her and Lucifer talking in low voices. He was already back from alerting Damon that we were on the way.

He must have sensed my presence because he cut off mid-sentence, stomped across the floor, and yanked the door open to glare at me. "We'll meet you downstairs in a moment."

Past his shoulder, Amy furiously wiped away the wetness on her cheeks as she turned her back to the door. Keisha held the baby, patting her back and humming low as Gabriel stood beside her with arms crossed. None of them were happy about leaving this place.

"Can I speak to you in private after I've delivered them?" I asked Lucifer.

"Why?"

I pointed a finger at the floor and the Fate below. "It's better if I don't explain, but it is important."

He arched a brow. "It better be."

The door slammed in my face. I blinked and returned downstairs, helping myself to a premade sandwich in one of the display cases. I snagged a soda to go with it.

Rad sat at one of the tables, toying with a plastic knife. In anyone else's hands, it would seem harmless. In his, it was as deadly as any metal blade. His chaos magic could drive it right through a heart or use it to slit open a throat.

His fingers manipulated it with ease as if he were playing his guitar. He was about as happy as the group upstairs.

I hurriedly chewed the sandwich while I kicked aside one of the chairs and plopped down. "I know the situation is not ideal, but what's really eating you?"

"How did we get here?"

"You've been along for the entire ride. You know how."

"I mean, you and I. How did we end up lapdogs for Lucifer?" He jabbed the knife's point into the top of the table, breaking off the tip. "First it was Maria, then the Noctefectors for me and the Bridge for you."

"There's nothing I'd like better than to return to Sweet Investigations and ignore all of this. Go back to how things were—helping humans and other supernaturals with their problems."

"Why don't we? Screw all of this. When do you and I get to do what we want?"

He knew the answer to that; he was just feeling pissy. I was right there with him. "I'm working on this for *us*." I didn't care who heard me. I am a demon, and that means I'm selfish. It was to be expected. "Whatever happens, I will make sure you and I have a chance. I can't predict the future or guarantee the outcome, but this is what I *can* offer—a chance for us to leave all of this behind and do what we want."

"Team Kali." It was said with a sharp level of discontent. He wanted to believe me, but he knew the odds as well as I did. "It will never be over, no matter what they want to believe."

"What do you mean?"

"You think all of this is random? That God, or whoever created the universe, would allow sin in the first place if he truly loved humans?"

A valid point; one I had considered many times. "So why do you think He did it?"

"Either He isn't as omniscient as everyone claims and didn't realize humans would go down this path, or..."

"He wanted them to," I finished.

"I'm tired of feeling like someone else is pulling the strings. Free will is a joke. We're in The Matrix, and someone is always writing a script that we're forced to act out."

This gave me pause. I sipped my soda. The movies depicted a fabricated reality and simulated world created by machines to deceive humans. Substitute God for the machines, and you had a similar world with angels and demons in place of secret agents.

The war between machines and humans might symbolize the war we faced. The oracle in that story was similar to Faron. A chill crept up my spine. "So, how do we go Neo on the matrix and break out?"

He gave me a forced grin. "You're the smart one. You tell me."

I finished the soda and tossed the cup and sandwich wrapper in the garbage. Hearing the others descend the stairs, I gestured for him to follow me to the office. "Let me think about it, but one thing we should do is try to be unpredictable."

He grabbed me by the hand and yanked me back, crushing me to his chest and kissing me. "Like this?" he asked with heavily lidded eyes.

My breathing picked up, and I huffed out a chuckle. "Yeah, like that." I kissed him back as ardently and then dragged him to the office.

Everyone was there now, including Bane, Frank, and Cole. The only one missing was Zayfeer. I was more than happy to leave him behind.

"Form a circle and hold hands," I instructed the group.

Lucifer gave Amy a peck on the forehead and brushed a hand over Azaria's head. "I'll catch up with you soon."

Her jaw was set, and she gave him a stiff "Be careful."

He faded from sight. I bit my lip to keep from reminding him that I needed a moment of his time. If he wanted to use me as a secret agent, he knew the importance of communication between us.

I pulled the ring from around my neck and stepped into the circle. "Ready?"

I didn't wait for confirmation, closing my eyes and sending us to the Institute.

abriss was waiting for us when we landed in the upstairs apartments area of the Institute. "I'll take things from here," she informed me. She gestured at Amy. "Follow me."

She waved a hand over the knob to Damon's chambers, and the lock clicked, the door opening.

What the hell?

I fell into step with Amy as the air witch as she carried her child and she and her entourage trailed after the head of the Fallen angels. Tabriss came to a full stop, pinning me with a glare as she motioned the others to enter. "I said, I've got this."

"Forgive me if I don't trust you enough to hand the most valuable cargo on the planet over without verifying your intent."

I stepped into the apartment. Damon's wood smoke smell and the magical residue from him living here sent ripples over my skin. The last time I'd been inside these walls, things between us had been…intense.

When *weren't* they, though?

Multiple sets of eyes flipped between me and Tabriss. She left the door open, indicating I should go. "Damon gave me this assignment."

"According to you," I countered. "I'll help Amy and the baby get settled before I check with him."

She advanced on me, getting in my face. "I am on your side, idiot."

Damon arrived at that moment. "Welcome to the Institute," he said smoothly to our guests.

Winking at Tabriss just to piss her off, I made a quick round of introductions. He'd already met Amy, but not Keisha, Gabriel, or the Fate and her…whatever Bane was.

Our apartments here aren't huge, and his main living area was too small for all of us. He signaled us to follow him. "We have our underground living facility ready for you."

"We do?" I stayed close to Amy and Azaria. "You never told me we had a basement."

"There are many things I haven't shared with you," he muttered out of the corner of his mouth. The look he flicked over his shoulder told me to shut up. *We'll talk about it later.*

You bet your demon ass we will. "I can't wait to see it," I said with false excitement.

Tabriss pushed past me as we filed past Damon's bedroom. "We don't need you tagging along. Don't you have the world to save?"

Her sarcasm and spite were thick. "Careful," I told her, "you sound jealous."

She snorted, claiming a spot next to Damon as he

stepped inside his study and ran a hand along one of the bookshelves. "Pathetic," she grumbled.

I was going to show her pathetic if she kept this up. The bookshelf slid back to reveal a secret doorway. My, oh my, my Bridge boss was full of surprises today.

The elevator would only hold five at a time. Damon sent Keisha, Gabriel, Bane, Faron, and Tabriss first.

When they disappeared, Damon smiled at Amy. "You'll be safe here."

"If Kali doesn't trust Tabriss," she said, stroking her daughter's hair, "neither do I."

Smart.

"Need I remind you," I added, "Tabriss once tried to take over the Institute and exterminate the Fallen."

Damon used his patient voice, but I felt his simmering annoyance lick up my spine. "I have spoken at length with her. She is stepping up, and I have given her this assignment to increase her confidence and leadership skills. I assure you, she can keep you safe and ensure your needs are met while you're here."

When did he turn into a used car salesman?

He pivoted to face Rad and Cole, who'd brought up the rear. "I assume you have better things to do than accompany us. I'll escort Amy and Azaria to their quarters." His eyes locked on mine. "Kali, wait for me in my office."

"Lucifer entrusted me with their safety," I asserted. "Where they go, I go."

The heat along my spine intensified. "While I appreciate your commitment to your job, I assure you I will handle this."

Butting heads with him was occasionally fun. We sparred with words and got under each other's skin. Right then, however, I was in full battering ram mode. "No can do." The elevator returned, and the doors opened. I stepped inside, and Amy followed. "I'll judge whether it's safe or not."

Cole stepped back. "I need to check in with my security people. I'll catch up with you later."

Rad gave me a questioning look. Did I want him to ignore Damon's orders?

I gestured for him to conform.

He wasn't happy but dipped his chin in deference to me, not Damon. "I'll be across the hall when you're ready for me," he said.

I barely kept the grin off my face. Across the hall was my apartment. I winked at him, letting him know he better be naked when I got back.

The drop to the underground level was quick, but Damon's seething under his classy suit made it feel twice as long. I had the distinct impression he wanted to turn me over his knee and spank me. That image was disturbing under any circumstance, and I shoved it away.

The basement was surprisingly nice. It had the feel of emptiness, though. I couldn't be sure when it had been built —during the initial construction of the building or at some point thereafter. Either way, I doubted anyone had used it since its inception.

The current space boasted modern furniture, granite countertops, and an impressive media center. Amy looked pleased. "This will do."

Tabriss, acting as her guide, led her to a bedroom that had been kitted out for a baby. Crib? Check. Changing table? Check. Immense toy chest? That, too.

"Whatever you need, you let me know," Tabriss insisted. "I'll handle it."

Faron stood in the hall. She crooked a finger at me. I held up one of my own to let her know I'd speak to her momentarily. Keisha gave her stamp of approval and then asked Tabriss where her room was. Tabriss continued the tour with her and Gabriel in tow.

Bane called to Faron. She slunk past me and off to the media center. Damon and I squared off in the doorway while Amy lowered her diaper bag to the floor inside the nursery and checked out a rocking chair. Damon lowered his voice. "When was the last time you slept, ate, or"—he sniffed the air—"showered?"

"Uh..." I covertly inhaled. Yep, no deodorant in the world was going to handle that stink. "Believe it or not, I've been busy."

"Hey, Kali?" Amy was wrestling with the zipper on the diaper bag. "Could use a hand here."

Grateful to escape Damon's overbearing energy that was about to turn fussy, I reached for it. She plopped the baby into my arms instead.

"I, uh... You mean..." Wow, I needed to work on my word stock. Definitely in need of food and sleep to get my brain back online. "Why don't you let me tackle that zipper?" I tried to return Azaria to her.

She gave me a curious scan. "She's a baby. She won't bite. Yet."

Azaria chewed on her fingers and made gurgling noises as she stared up at my face. Her dark brown eyes were nearly black. They reminded me of fathomless voids. Black holes.

I felt some sort of trippy falling sensation.

"May I be of assistance?" Damon asked, snapping me out of it.

Azaria giggled. I narrowed my eyes at her.

Amy waved him off. "Go do whatever archdemons do. We've got this."

Her casual brush-off made me like the witch even more.

Damon's jaw clenched, but he smiled and gave a slight bow. "Kali? My office when you're done."

"Yes, of course, sir."

I'm going to make you pay for that, he said in my head.

He and I were always on unequal footing with each other. He'd been my boss since we were still in Spain a century ago. It was hard to look at him differently.

But I wasn't the same employee, the same demon that I'd been all these years. A lot had changed. We still weren't on equal footing, and although I teased him by calling him 'boss,' we both knew in the hierarchy of things, I was no longer a simple underling.

Demons are big on hierarchy, just like angels.

Which made me think about Tabriss and Michael. Humans were under the misconception that archangels were the highest level of divine beings, right under God, but that wasn't true. There were legions of angels higher up the heavenly ladder, and before she had been incarnated as Mary Magdalene, Tabriss had been one of them.

My spiritual mother was once a beloved, divine entity

higher than Lucifer Morningstar. This fact boggled my mind.

Azaria patted my cheek, demanding my attention. I'd never held a child before, outside of my younger sister. It was a fuzzy memory, having occurred three hundred years ago. Since then, I'd never had the chance, nor the desire, to be around children. I found them...messy.

However, some deep-seated, instinctual part of me kicked in. Without realizing what I was doing, I began gently bouncing her on my hip. She continued to put her palm on my cheek with such tenderness that it felt like a kiss.

I sensed no inherent angel magic in her, and the thought made me stop bouncing. Why was that? She was supposed to be the most powerful of magic beings on the planet at the moment. I should be able to sense something.

Staring into those dark abysses, I probed her lightly with my magic. She giggled again as if I were tickling her.

Amy smiled, wiggling her fingers in a manner similar to Keisha's. Her air magic nipped at my skin as she used a bit of it to free the zipper. "She likes you."

Did she? For a moment, the idea caused a funny flutter in my chest. My lips turned up in an involuntary, goofy grin.

"Have you and Rad thought about having kids?" Amy asked.

My mouth fell open. I shut it before I said 'uh' again. "No."

"Why not?"

I almost said, 'duh.' "Our lives aren't conducive to having kids, and his chaos magic is...well, chaotic. He's an anomaly —his half-human side shouldn't be able to control his demon side." I shrugged. "Carrying a baby with chaos magic to term is nearly impossible."

That was the sanitized version of *no way in fucking Hell*. We were both damned, as was this world if Azaria didn't save it, and I was about as baby-oriented as a gerbil. Scratch that. Even gerbils were capable of taking care of their offspring. Me? That was laughable.

"Do you think having a kid with Lucifer is conducive to raising a family?"

"Fair point, but you have a leg up on me—you're Fallen. You act about as normal for a non-human as I've seen."

She hauled out a diaper. "Thank you?" she said uncertainly.

I realized Azaria's jumper felt full under her bottom, resting on my arm. I also caught the scent of urine. Great.

I was about to hand her to her mother when she placed her chubby fingers against my lips. Her eyes went a strange amber color, and I felt like I'd been struck by lightning from the end of my hair down to the tips of my toes.

She filled my head with three different visions, one right after the other. Each filled me with abject fear.

They came so fast and so intensely that I felt like I was spinning in the abyss created by her eyes. I didn't know which way was up or down, and all sensation of gravity evaporated.

The air in my lungs was sucked out into that nothingness. My bones began to dissolve. I had no voice box, no fingers, no beating heart.

And then everything snapped back into place.

Amy was talking and smiling as if nothing had happened. She reached for her daughter and lifted her out of my hands. "You can practice with Azaria anytime. I mean, as long as we're here, if you want to hang out...?"

Keisha blasted into the room. "This place isn't bad," she announced. "How long do you think we'll have to stay?"

They were both looking at me while I tried to remember how to breathe. To figure out how gravity worked again. Luckily, Amy had hold of Azaria because my hands and fingers didn't seem to want to function. Nor did my brain. "Huh?"

The two women exchanged a look. Amy winked at Keisha. "She's never held a baby before."

Keisha playfully punched my arm. "Got your hormones stirred up, didn't it? Badass Kali Sweet with a baby. Wonders will never cease."

Maddy picked that moment to pop her head in. "Wait, what? Did I just hear that right? Kali's pregnant?"

Still reeling from the visions, I stumbled for the doorway, shaking my head at her. Something in my expression must have warned her that I needed air. She grabbed my arm and studied me. "If you need a babysitter," she said to Amy, "I'm available."

I staggered down the hall to the elevator. Faron and Bane were waiting beside it.

Faron tilted her head at me. "Are you sick?"

I locked down my thoughts, pushing the visions behind a solid steel door in my brain. Punching the button, I was relieved when the doors parted immediately. "Yes. It's probably contagious. You should take the next ride."

Maddy slid inside with me, and I closed the doors on their mutually suspicious faces.

"I can't believe you're pregnant, and you didn't tell me,"

she whined. "First a dog, now a kid? What's gotten into you? Does Dru know? Oh my god, he's going to throw a fang when he hears."

I leaned against the wall as it whisked us up to Damon's apartment. "The devil," I said. "He's fucking ruined everything."

21

 *M*y mother had been a Seer. I'd never had the gift.

Now, I was glad I hadn't.

Except Azaria hadn't been rocking any angel mojo. I hadn't detected magic of any kind running through her system. How had she pushed those visions—premonitions? —into my mind?

Rad was playing his guitar—naked—on my bed when Maddy and I burst into my apartment.

He jumped up, and Maddy gawked. "Damn."

I staggered to the nearest chair. Ignoring her, Rad tossed the guitar on the bed and approached me. "What's wrong?"

"Like you don't know," Maddy said, closing the door behind her before joining us. "Do you need saltine crackers? Herbal tea? Pickles and ice cream?"

"Go away," I groaned, rubbing my temples.

Rad frowned at her, then at me. "What is she talking

about?" His eyes grew wide as the words sank in. "Wait. You're not...?"

Pregnant, no. Homicidal? Getting close. "Of course not. Maddy, find Salmad. I need him."

She let go of an Oscar-worthy sigh. "Fine." She marched to the door. "I'll get Kirill, too."

"I don't need a doctor. Just the priest."

"Whatever."

She stomped out, and Rad took hold of my chin and forced me to look at him. "What's going on? What happened in the basement?"

"I saw... I'm not sure what I saw." I held my stomach, a dull pain throbbing in my gut. "But Lucifer is not being honest with me."

"That surprises you?"

It was more than that. If what Azaria had shown me would come to pass, it meant that...

The door banged open. Frank rushed in. He held out my father's book. "Read this passage."

"What are you doing with that?"

He glanced at Rad's naked body and gave a sharp squeak. "Have I interrupted something?"

"Yes," Rad said.

"No." I forced myself to stand. My legs wobbled. "You didn't ask permission to take my book."

He waved me off. "Your father's work is impressive, and I learned something about the prophecy." He held the volume out to me, tapping his finger at a section. "Read this."

It was all Greek to me, literally. "I can't. I don't know the language."

"You're a demon. Translate it."

"This may come as a surprise to you, but it doesn't work that way. I know Italian, some Spanish, and some curse words in French. That's it."

He adjusted his glasses with frustration. "Demons and angels can translate any language that exists. You're not trying."

I jerked the book from his grip. "I've never heard of such a thing. Maybe as a Fallen you can do that, but as far as I know, I don't have an internal translation app I can turn on whenever needed." I looked to Rad for confirmation, and he nodded.

"English, French, and a little Italian that I learned in order to woo her in Queen Maria's court," he told Frank. "That's the extent of my lexicon."

Frank snatched the book back, flipping it open to the previous page and tapping his finger on the section again. "The prophecy. About Azaria."

I wanted to pick him up and throw him across the room. "We already know about the prophecy. Your kind gets to be angels again. Paradise is restored. Yada, yada, yada." Except in the vision Azaria had jammed into my head, that wasn't happening, thanks to her father. *El porca miseria.*

Frank sighed as if dealing with unruly children. "That's the prophecy that made it into the Bible. These are visions your mother saw that your father recorded. They didn't make the cut."

I glanced at the text, even though I couldn't decipher it. "What does it say?"

Salmad, Kirill, and Damon entered without knocking. "What's this we hear about"—Kirill cut off at the site of Rad. "Jesus God, put some damn clothes on!"

"My apartment is apparently Grand Central Station," I grumbled as Rad reluctantly pulled on a pair of cargo pants.

Damon's face was ashen. The corners of his mouth were tight, and a crease I hadn't noticed before between his brows looked like a canyon. "Are you with child?"

I sat in the chair with a thud. "No, for the love of all that's evil, I'm *not* pregnant!"

All three of them looked relieved. Rad squeezed my shoulder.

"You don't need medical help, then?" Kirill asked, his keen eyes sweeping over me for any apparent illness or injury.

"She doesn't look good," Frank said. "Maybe you should give her a checkup."

"It's not physical," I argued.

Kirill continued his visual probe. "Are you magic sick?"

I'd never heard of such a thing. "What's that?"

"You've been traipsing through different dimensions and hanging out with powerful divine beings. As a demon, that can take its toll."

"It's not that," I assured him.

"Then why did you call us here?" Sal asked.

I rubbed a hand down my face. "I only wanted to speak to you."

"About what?"

"It's good you're all here," Frank interjected. "I found something in this book by John of Patmos that we need to discuss and bring to Lucifer's attention."

"Yeah, no," I said. "Not him, not yet. Tell me what it says first."

He read it aloud in Greek first, and I saw Damon's face go

even paler. He was the one who was going to need a doctor again before this day was over.

"Lovely," I griped. "English, please."

"And the prophesied One of Worlds, given to them by the Almighty, the Protector, the I am, the—"

"Yeah, we get it. God is great and has nine hundred and fifty names." I rolled a finger in a hurry-up gesture. "What's the important point?"

He gave me a chastising glance. *"The Beast will rise up in all its evil glory and slay the One."*

"We already handled the apocalypse," I told him. "The Four Horsemen, the Beast, all that."

"In this passage, the One refers to the entity that will unite the Fallen with Heaven. The Beast refers to the demon who will sabotage the Fallen's quest to do so."

It got far too quiet in the room, all eyes landing on me.

There are times in a demon's life when Hell looks like a vacation. This was one of those times. "It's not me," I insisted. "I'm on your side, remember? It must be Tabriss."

"Why her?" Salmad challenged. "Why do you insist on seeing her in the worst possible light?"

The problem was, I knew it *wasn't* her. My visions of the future and this prophecy lined up like two magnets snapping together.

Except for one crucial fact: it wasn't a demon who sabotaged the quest. It was—

Lucifer appeared out of thin air. "We need to talk," he said to me.

Oh, goodie. "We sure do." I motioned the others out. "If you'll excuse us."

Rad and Damon were the last to leave, each throwing a glance back at me. I gave nothing away.

Frank left my father's journal on the chair. I flipped it closed and sat on top of it. "You have some explaining to do, king of Hell."

He gave me his classic *fuck you* smolder. "My daughter likes you, I'm told. It's the only reason I'm sparing your worthless life at this moment."

He wanted to play that game? Fine. Bring it on.

I stood, going toe-to-toe with him. "And she's the only reason I haven't revealed your evil plan to this entire Institute. Start talking and convince me why I shouldn't do it right now."

"*My* evil plan? You're the one double- and triple-crossing me. I put my faith in you, and this is how you repay it?"

"What are you talking about?"

His reply was to grab my arm, and suddenly, my molecules were being whisked through space.

At first, it had been a novelty, but now I was tired of it. This was more than my meat suit could handle on a regular basis.

Where we emerged was a post-apocalyptic dimension. A marble city sat half buried in sand; the buildings, statues, and obelisk markers surrounding us resembled gravestones.

Whatever had happened here, we appeared to be in the center of ground zero.

Shit. Azaria's vision filled my mind like tracing paper sliding over my current view. In her version, however, not one of these elements was left.

Nothing moved but drifting sand. I kept an eye out for

Micheal, but all was silent and creepy. "Where are we? What is the place?"

"This is where my brother buried most of my friends and family." Lucifer pointed at the marble columns, crumbling buildings, and eroded statues jutting. "This is the City of Lost Angels. A prison world Michael created. I've rescued all of them now, and here it sits, empty, vacant, waiting."

It didn't take a rocket scientist to understand what he was planning. I shook off the heavy jetlag of our latest trip. "I haven't betrayed you."

"According to Faron, you will."

"Faron told you I'm your greatest ally. Have you forgotten that?"

"Things changed. You've made other decisions."

Had I? If so, it was not a conscious action.

Azaria's visions—what she had shown me—I hadn't even thoroughly dissected the first one, much less had a minute to comprehend the second and third. "If you think I'm going to betray you, why not kill me? Why put me here?"

"You might be useful to me as a sacrifice."

I scoffed. "Who do you think would want me?"

"My brother wants you very much. While you are cunning and strategic, I wonder why you, out of all the demons, have enticed him so."

"I realize you're under an immense amount of stress right now. He's got your principalities, Lilith is threatening Amy, and you still haven't finished raising your army, but sticking me here defeats everything we've been working for when it comes to sabotaging Michael. I bound myself to that bastard for you. I got Frank free from him for you. I am the one who figured out that he's been working with Lilith to defeat you."

I pounded a fist against my chest. "Oh, and I'm also the one who has made him believe I'm on his side so I have a way of feeding him the wrong information. Who's going to do that for you now, Lucifer?"

In all my years, never did I imagine yelling at the supreme ruler of Hell. But I was tired—physically, emotionally, and mentally—and let's be honest, I never make good choices when I'm hangry.

He was itching for a fight, and that's probably the only reason he didn't smite me right there. It wasn't because he wanted to use me as a sacrifice; he simply needed to lash out at someone, and I was his whipping post. "I don't need you. I don't need anyone. I can handle this on my own."

I trudged over to a broken piece of marble and plunked down, massaging the back of my neck. "Be my guest. All I want is for my life to return to the way it used to be. To be rid of this daily dose of archangels up my ass trying to force me to help them. Give me investigations. Let me worry about demons taking advantage of humans. Devise plots to defeat them. I want to stake vampires in the heart and burn witches at the stake. But you know what? No matter what outcome this leads to, I don't get what I want. So I surrender." I held up my hands. "Leave me here. Maybe I'll finally get some rest and a break from listening to your whiny ass complain about your brother."

He did strike me then, not with his magic, but with his fist.

A right hook to my jaw sent me to the ground. I spit blood from my split lip into the sand and watched it dissolve. Laughing, I rolled onto my back and stared at the roiling clouds overhead. "Feel better?"

He paced several feet away, shaking out his hand. "Oddly, yes. Get up."

"So you can sucker-punch me again? Hard pass. I'm gonna lay here and stare at the sky. You've broken me. Happy? Go back to your family, and good luck with the coming war."

He stomped up to me, grabbed the front of my shirt, and hauled me up far enough that he could hammer me with his fist again. Then, he released me, and I tumbled to the ground as he vanished.

My nose was broken, and a few of my teeth rattled as I adjusted my jaw. At least I had peace for the first time in days. I forced myself to my feet, wiped blood off with my sleeve, and studied my surroundings. "There better be something to eat," I yelled, trudging toward the nearest building.

What appeared before me wasn't the four-course meal I wanted.

In fact, it looked like *I* was on the menu.

"*Alciscor*." Lilith licked her lips as her gaze devoured me. Her thumb rubbed the edge of a dagger in her hand. Two hellhounds flanked her. "So good to see you again."

erde. This was almost my version of paradise until she showed up. Did I want to know what she wanted?

No. No, I didn't.

Alciscor was a name Lilith used for me, based on a similar Latin term that meant *to avenge.* Because of her power and status in the demon world, I should have bowed my head and greeted her appropriately. I didn't. "Wish I could say the same."

She quirked a brow and stalked me, her nostrils flaring at the scent of my blood. Her black hair fell in perfect waves around her shoulders. Her skin was impeccable, her almond-shaped eyes as dark as Azaria's. "Did he do this to you, my pet?"

I was done playing games, and I was nobody's pet. My desire to get back to Rad, Cole, and the others hadn't dimmed, but damn if I didn't need a break. "What do you want?"

Her hounds, as tall as my chest, sniffed me. At my tone, each of them peeled back their lips and showed me their fangs.

Sharp, very pointed fangs.

I exposed my own teeth, letting them know I could bite, too.

The tip of her dagger traced the outline of my jaw and slid down my neck to the base of my throat. "What has he done to you to make you lose your spark?"

My *spark*? Was this some New Age mumbo-jumbo? Had Lilith become enlightened? I didn't respond, noting that the dagger was too damn close for comfort.

She smiled slyly. "Your blood smells of Michael."

No sense in pretending otherwise. "I'm bloodbound to him."

"Why would you do such a senseless thing?"

"To save those I care about."

She sneered. "Humans?"

"And Demons. If Paradise comes, we'll cease to exist."

"That's why I'm here." She removed the dagger point from my skin and waved it around, indicating our surroundings. "Do you know what this place was?"

"Lucifer says it's the Lost City of Angels."

"Before that, this was Eden."

I scanned the landscape, searching for any indication it had previously been the famed Biblical garden. I saw nothing to indicate that, and Lilith wasn't exactly known for her honesty. On the other hand, why would she lie? "Doesn't look like much now."

The hounds backed off so she could stroll in a circle around me, using the dagger to touch me in various places.

She ran the tip down one arm, around my lower back, and up the other arm before standing in front of me again. She pressed her rack to mine and searched my face as if she might find the answer to her salvation there.

Good luck with that.

"I'm raising an army," she purred, "and I want you to join me."

"I'm sort of all joined out." The dagger was between our stomachs, and while I preferred it didn't get buried in mine, I didn't get the feeling she planned to use it. "The archangels beat you to it. They've both enlisted my help, and I have no choice but to fulfill my bargain with Michael. However, doing so will make sure at least some demons survive."

Hopefully, not you.

She touched the end of my nose, and the broken cartilage snapped, righting itself. I barked a yell and stumbled backward, grabbing it.

A cloth appeared in her hand, and she tossed it at me to wipe the blood away. "What if we send the angels back to Heaven," she said, "and we take over the Earth?"

My jaw still hurt, but her magic was healing my nose. My own magic was lending a hand.

I cleaned myself up and shoved the bloody cloth into my back pocket. I didn't trust her not to use it against me somehow down the road. "That's not going to happen. There's a prophecy—"

"I know about the prophecy. There have been many such things since time began that have never come true because of beings like you and I. There are many timelines, *alciscor,* and we have choices."

I wasn't going anywhere, so I figured I might as well hear

her out. I just wish I had something to eat while she talked. "Like what?"

"The key to stopping our demise resides in the Bridge Institute under your care now."

She knew about that, huh? "Lucifer has a Fate with him. She knew what you were planning the moment you put it into place. His wife and daughter are off-limits. He's put me here for that very reason because he doesn't trust me after Michael forced me into the bloodbond. He wrongly believes that I moved his family to the bunker to kill them myself."

"And would you? To save us?"

Not her, but it was best I didn't divulge that fact. "Going up against Lucifer is a suicide mission."

"Allowing him to reunite the Fallen with Heaven is as well, is it not?"

"Fun fact—he doesn't like me, and he can destroy me with half a thought."

"Yet, you still live." She gave me that sly smile again. "You and I are on the same side, and with my protection, he won't be able to touch you."

"You can't win against the archangels."

The old Lilith would have lashed out at me, but the new version seemed exceptionally confident as she strode to one of the broken monuments, hopping up on it. "Alone?" Her voice rang out over the area. "No. But with my army..." She swept the dagger through the air in a semi-circle around her. The energy pulsed, and I gasped as thousands of demons came into view.

They muttered and snarled and shifted from foot to foot. Some were bipedal, others on all fours. They sported tough, wrinkled skin, elongated claws, and horns. Bulging eyes glared at me, and noses flared as they scented me. Some bore weapons, others were weapons in and of themselves.

A horror movie come to life. The stench of sulfur hit my nose, and I eased my way backward, keeping an eye on them. Previously, I'd taken on a dozen or so attackers at once, but this many? There was no way I would survive if she gave the word for them to kill me.

"I have a plan," she purred, jumping down beside me. "I want you to be my general."

I saw the future again, not because of Azaria's vision, but thanks to my imagination. Thousands of demons covering the Earth and consuming humans.

Bloody, brutal extinction.

And then what? Would they turn on each other when there were no humans left?

Azaria's vision fell again like a filter over everything, this time making more sense. Her father stood—a giant in all his Lightbringer glory—on the edge of the world, cradling her lifeless body in one arm. The sword of Michael was in his other hand. But where was Amy in the vision?

On my knees before him, I bowed my head, waiting for the blade to remove it from my neck. Nothing was left; Lucifer had scorched the entire world to rid it of the demon pestilence that had taken over.

More than that, he'd ended the source of all suffering and was about to take the final act of retribution— against me.

For I was the Beast who'd risen up and killed the savior of the Fallen. I'd killed Azaria.

"My legion can be yours," Lilith crooned, pushing a

strand of hair from my face like a mother. "Work with me, *alciscor*, and I will give you everything."

Her army seemed to move as one, closing in another step. If I said no, would they tear me limb from limb? Eat my heart? Take me to Hell and torture me for eternity?

She wasn't giving me much of a choice, but everything was a negotiation. "I have a request," I said. "Two, actually."

A pause. Her patience and enlightened self were growing thin. "I'm listening."

"I want Michael's sword." The memory of how good it felt in my hand caused my palm to heat. Even Volante had felt the attraction to it. I wished she was with me now, and I tried to remember where I'd left her. I was exhausted beyond my limits if I'd lost track of my beloved whip.

"That's a substantial request."

"I'll need it if I am to go up against him or Lucifer, and that's assured if you're rising against them."

She hesitated, then faced me and smiled. Either she was confident she would get it, or she was bluffing. "Done. And the second?"

"Dinner. Steak—rare—and fries, with cheesecake for dessert. Preferably back on Earth with my friends."

"Another sizable request."

"Compared to taking out the archangels and Fallen? This is peanuts. If you can't provide either, you're not strong enough to win the war."

"A test?" She chucked me on the chin. Her hellhounds showed me their fangs again.

I snarled back. I'd slaughtered plenty of their kind, and my demon was done being intimidated. "Call it whatever you like, but those are my terms if you want my help."

She snapped her fingers, and the next thing I knew, I was in the Institute's cafeteria with a full-course steak meal in front of me.

When Damon strode in and yelled, "What the hell, Kali?" I glanced up from shoveling in the medium-rare piece of meat.

"You need better wards." I swallowed and sucked down some fries. "And once those are in place, we need to talk."

It took some serious negotiating with Alexandru, the king of the Chicago vampires, but Damon managed to get Victoria, the strongest witch I knew outside of Amy, to his office.

Victoria had once been in our dungeons but had petitioned Dru to be moved to the Chicago House. He didn't like having her there, but thanks to me, she was a vampire now, and he had a responsibility to each and every one of them.

Dressed to the nines in a silk suit with a red ascot, Dru was the sexiest vampire in the world. Not by my standards but by Maddy's and most of his followers. Thanks to the newest addition to the House, an influencer from one of the social media platforms, they had a monthly vampire ezine called *Lust*. Dru was featured in every issue.

While I was his queen, we shared no romantic relationship. It was only business. But damn. He was a fine male as he stood in the room, staring me down with an intensity that said he wanted to strip me naked and discipline me for making him deal with the witch. Looked like Damon would have to get in line for that spanking. "You said it was an emergency."

My blood had snapped to attention the moment he'd

stepped onto the property. We shared something wholly different than anything I'd ever experienced. We'd exchanged blood—not because I'd wanted to, but in order to survive, certain concessions had been necessary. That bond gave us certain leverage with each other, as well. Hence, asking for this favor. "Good to see you, too, my lord," I said, giving him a cocky grin. "It's been too long."

Dru's irritation slid away, his keen senses instantly alert at my sweet words. "Where are my manners?" He strode forward, took my hand, and kissed my palm, his eyes never leaving mine. As his lips brushed my skin, he inhaled deeply and smiled at me from beneath his dark brows. "I am glad to see you are well."

That was debatable. I gave a mock curtsey. "And you, my lord."

Damon's impatient magic flared, goosing mine. *Get on with it.*

"I apologize for interrupting your day." I left my hand in Dru's grip, not disliking the thrum of his power flowing up my arm and into my chest. So much darker and richer than the tartness of angelic mojo. "I'm in need of Victoria's spell-work to enhance the Institute's wards, and it is indeed an emergency."

Victoria spat on the ground, her wild red hair shorter than the last time I'd seen her. "Go screw yourself. I got nothing out of our last deal."

When she was human, she'd been a powerful witch and leader of the *Satrina Arcanum*. I wanted her for more than the wards, but baby steps. "You have a reputation now that rivals mine when it comes to outsmarting archangels," I reminded her. "And Dru was kind enough to grant your petition to move to the House."

She raised her manacled hands. "I'm still a prisoner."

Slipping past Dru, I faced her. She'd lost much of the crazed manic energy she'd had when I'd first met her. I hoped her devotion to another queen was still intact. "I've spoken to Lilith. She has a job for you."

Interest flared behind her flat eyes, but she quickly squelched it. "You're lying."

"There's a New World order coming, Vicky. Do this tiny favor for me, and I'll make sure you have a prominent position in it."

The two males behind me and the guards on either side of her stiffened. None knew what I was talking about, but instinct told them to be wary.

"That's where you made your mistake," Vicky said. "As soon as you say 'tiny,' I know it will be a major favor. I also know you hate Lilith. You would never work with her."

"When it comes to manipulating certain outcomes, I have many bed partners." I winked at her. "The chessboard has been rearranged, and I'll work with whomever I need to in order to save demons, vampires, and even you, Victoria."

My sincerity must have registered. Curiosity replaced her hesitancy. "Go on."

"The spell you used to cloak me from Michael—you strengthened it to cover the Institute and the Fallen."

"Yeah, so?"

"It's no longer effective. Has it weakened because you're not here, or did you purposely set it to fail at some point?"

Her face blanched. "My magic is not weak."

"Then, you admit that you intentionally designed the spell to fail?"

"Surely not," Dru said, moving to stand beside me. "That would endanger your queen and be seen as an act of treason."

Punishable by death. Permanent death in the Undead world.

Vicky had often claimed she didn't fear dying—Lilith was in Hell, after all, and she'd get to be with her. But she preferred to raise the mother of demons and let her party it up on Earth. That had always been Vicky's goal.

While that might still be buried under the current self-righteous attitude, she didn't show it. "Anything is better than being a prisoner."

Vicky had gone Zen on me before my last showdown with Michael. How could I motivate her now without giving too much away?

Michael and Lucifer had learned that threats only went so far in motivating me, and both had switched to offering me rewards instead. It was time I turned the tables and did the same with her. "I'll grant you your freedom in exchange for a simple reupping of the magic."

Stunned silence smacked into me.

"You can't be serious," Dru said.

Everyone around me would have to put considerable trust in me going forward. I was going to say and do things that made them doubt my allegiances, my cunning, and my intelligence. "Dead serious. The battles are only beginning. The war we face is beyond our comprehension. We must reinforce the wards so we can speak more freely, or any planning we do is moot."

Everything in Vicky stilled. Everything but the wheels in her brain. Even the most hardened criminal imprisoned for life can flip over like a dog and show you their belly when the carrot of freedom is dangled in front of them. "I don't believe you," she said.

"If I were in your shoes, I wouldn't either. Things have changed, however. For all of us. I'm looking for new allies, and I'd like you to be one of them."

The deafening silence fell again. Dru and Damon were telepathically trying to get my attention, demanding to know what I was doing. I pushed them to the back of my mind, letting them buzz like bees around a hive while I stayed focused on her.

Leaning toward me, she sniffed. I forced myself not to back up. Her vampire senses picked up the scent of sand, hellhounds, and the queen she loved to worship. Probably a tinge of sulfur and brimstone, as well.

Her nostrils flared, and her eyes went wide. "Did she ask for me?"

An echo of Tabriss's previous question about Michael. Love made us stupid, devotion even more so. "Why do you think I'm here requesting you reinforce the wards? I can't give you her message until I'm sure a certain entity isn't listening." I pointed toward the heavens.

She knew I was talking about Michael.

The manacles jangled as she held out her hands. The offer of freedom had snagged her interest, but the idea that Lilith had a message for her made her sit up and beg. "What are you waiting for? Do it."

23

"*A*re you mad?" Dru demanded, halting the closest guard from unlocking them. "What is going on, Kali?"

"I'd like to know, too," Damon bellowed. "Have you switched allegiances?"

Did no one trust me? "All in good time, gentlemen." I gave each a pointed stare. "Everything will become clear soon."

Dru's attention shifted to Vicky with reluctance. "Do not test me, underling. I won't hesitate to put you down."

She curled a lip, revealing a fang—a clear act of rebellion. "You don't scare me."

"He should," Damon snapped, easing down on the edge of his desk and crossing his arms. "We all should. You're a powerful witch-vampire hybrid, but you're no match for him." He looked her over. "Or me."

"Or me," I added. "Which is why you should join us rather than fight us."

"Yeah, yeah, whatever. I'm not a fool." She shook her hands and the heavy linked chain between them. "Get these off."

I dipped my chin at the guard with the key. Although I was his queen, he slid a questioning peek at Dru.

Dru sighed in disgust. "Do it."

The chain and iron manacles clanged to the floor. Vicky cracked her knuckles and took a seat on Damon's sofa. "A drink, please. Something to eat, too."

Damon grunted. "You'll be lucky to—"

"I'll ask Neve to bring up refreshments," I interrupted, using Damon's phone to call her.

We had to wait for Vicky to drink a quart of blood and eat a rare piece of meat before she'd do my bidding. While the guards kept an eye on her, Dru and Damon pulled me aside and began interrogating me.

"I can't explain yet," I insisted. "But know this—Lucifer, Michael, or even Lilith could yank me out of here at any moment. They could kill me. You have to be prepared to make some uncomfortable but strategic sacrifices if you're to survive."

"I'm not sacrificing you," Damon said softly.

Dru ran a hand down my arm. "I refuse to, as well."

Damon glanced over his shoulder at Vicky, who was polishing off her meal. "Does Lucifer know you're here?" he murmured at me.

I shook my head. "He believes I'm going to betray him because the Fate said I would. That's bullshit, but he believes her over me."

"The Fate?" Dru queried.

"Faron is one of three," I explained, "and she's keeping

an eye on all of us. She can read our intentions and predict outcomes."

"Why would she lie about your intentions?" Dru asked.

"Because she has her own agenda," Damon said, catching onto my theory.

I nodded. "What happens to her and the others like her —gods, goddesses, the whole works—if Lucifer succeeds? Will they be eradicated like demons? I mean, who needs fate if your destiny is to die peacefully in Paradise? No matter your choices, it's all rainbows and puppy dogs. And what better way to ensure you aren't expunged from this world than to sabotage him?"

Damon strode behind his desk and punched a button on his landline. "Neve, send Salmad to my office immediately."

Setting aside her empty plate, Vicky downed the last of the blood and rubbed her hands together. Her eyes closed, and her short hair began to tremble, strands straightening and lifting as if on a breeze.

The hair on the back of my neck rose to attention.

"Why do we need the priest?" Dru asked Damon quietly.

My boss and I were on the same page. "Sal will have a theory about the Fate's fate," I told him, "but we can't alert Faron to the fact we suspect she's a plant."

Damon sat in his chair. "Working for Michael or Lilith?"

I moved to stare out the window at Lake Michigan. As usual, it was more gray than blue, even though the sun shone on it. "Why not both? When Cole and I were at the carnival, it felt like several magics had been braided together. More than just Michael's and Lilith's. What if hers was the other one I felt?"

"There's your problem," Vicky said. We all turned to

her, and she flipped open her eyes. "The original wards that you put on the place"—she pointed at Damon—"formed the initial barrier, and the amount of angel energy inside the Institute has been weakening it in spots. There's too much divine power building up under your demonic layers. Angelic forces outside the Institute are battering the spell I placed on top of it." She used her hands to mimic two forces smacking against each other. "It's a powder keg. All the pressure inside and out is causing cracks and allowing Michael's power to seep into the structure and foundation."

"Can you fix it?" I asked.

She made a face as her keen eyes shifted to mine. "When I look at your energy, it's translucent and filmy. You're more spirit than flesh and blood. You carry a coating of other dimensions—Hell and others that reek of angels but aren't Heaven."

"Can you fix the wards?" Damon demanded, bringing her back on point.

She rolled her eyes. "Your best bet would be to remove the angels from here. They're weakening your wards simply by being inside these walls."

A knock sounded. Salmad entered with Frank on his heels. "May I be of assistance?"

I jutted my chin at the principality. "What's he doing here?"

Frank pushed up his glasses and showed me my father's book. "There's more that I think you should be made aware of."

The door was still open, and Rad barreled in, nearly knocking both men over. "You're back."

In his eyes, I could see his concern, mixed with irritation that I hadn't come to him. "I am. Can you do me a favor?"

He marched forward and kissed me, leaving me breathless. "You know I would do anything for you."

I ran my hand down his cheek. "I need Volante and Cole, but I need you to be sneaky about it. Lucifer can't know I'm here."

This seemed to relieve his annoyance. He glanced at Vicky. She had closed her eyes again and was murmuring snippets of a spell under her breath. I hoped it had to do with the wards and not that she was cursing me. Rad faced Dru. "Do I know what the two of you are doing here?"

I placed a hand on his arm. "Helping us save demondom."

He quirked a brow. "New word?"

"New word for a New World order."

He released me reluctantly, and I could feel the tug-of-war inside him. The room was packed with powerful supernatural males, a vampire-witch hybrid, a priest, and an angel. He didn't trust any of them. He only trusted me.

Score one for Team Kali. "I'll be back," he said.

Something about what Vicky had said tickled my mind. "Victoria," I said, "does my ability to dimension hop make it easier for Michael and Lilith to yank me out of the Institute?"

She cracked open an eye. "Of course. Like them, you can now travel through time and space without recourse."

"Can you put an additional ward over her to prevent her from being snatched from this room?" Damon asked.

"I need to anchor her to a living entity, not a room."

Damon and I exchanged a glance. In my head, he asked

permission. I granted it. He nodded at Vicky. "Anchor her to me."

A tickling, prickling sensation raced over my skin, and an intimate ward meant only for me snapped into place. Body armor. A shield.

My inner demon purred at the feeling of being connected to Damon's archdemon's power. She latched onto him and sank her claws into his dominance and supremacy.

He grunted as he felt it, too, and his dark eyes glittered like stars in a midnight sky. He internally grabbed my demon around the neck and forced her to her knees.

She rebelled, and I did, too, coming to my physical feet. "What...the...hell..." I wheezed, clawing at my throat.

"What are you doing to her?" Dru demanded, reaching out to me.

Damon released his grip, and the vice around my neck vanished. "Should you try to overpower me or force me to do anything I wish not to, you'll find yourself in an even worse position," he warned.

I assured Dru I was fine, then gave Damon a saucy wink even though I raged inside. "Aww, that's cute. Be careful, archdemon. You are one powerful SOB, but I have angelic mojo running in my veins."

"Don't get cocky," he warned. "Being bloodbound to Michael only makes you weak."

We'd see about that. Clearing my throat, I snatched the book from Frank. "Prove to me you're on our side."

He made a flustered noise and glanced at Salmad, Damon, and back to me. "I don't know what you're asking. I'm translating your father's book for you. Why would I do that if I wasn't?"

"Demons are accused of being selfish, and we are, but I haven't met an angel yet who wasn't also in the game for themselves. Did Michael kidnap you, or was that all a ruse? Are the other principalities in on it?"

My goal was to keep him off-center. It seemed to be working. "I didn't even know this was going on," he insisted. "I was minding my own business, and then you came along and screwed it up."

"What did Lilith offer you to help Michael?"

He took off his glasses and chuckled dryly. "I have no idea what you're talking about. I'm not working with Lilith, or Michael, or even Lucifer. All I'm trying to do is survive. I've been yanked into this daytime drama and given no options about what *I* want, so call me selfish if you want, but you're the one who insists I take part in this war."

I tapped the book on my leg and then tossed it on the desk to Damon. "I think this is propaganda. Michael handed it over far too freely. Whatever is written in there is meant to misdirect us."

Frank returned his glasses to his nose, peering at me as if I were a few claws short of being a full demon. "That makes no sense from what I've translated so far. If anything, it supports you."

Damon sat forward. "Demons, you mean?"

"Not demons," Sal interrupted. "Kali."

"How so?" Damon asked.

Sal frowned at Vicky and Dru as if he wished not to respond in their presence.

Vicky finished chanting, and I felt a firm snap of power lock in. "The best I can do at this point is to ward this office," she said, reaching for her glass. "Can I get another shot of blood?"

"This office is warded from Michael and Lucifer?" I confirmed.

"And the Fate," she added.

I glanced at my boss. "Shall we test it?"

He made a go-ahead gesture.

Rad and Cole burst in at that moment. Rad tossed Volante to me, and she wrapped around my arm of her own accord.

Damn, it was good to have her back, and yet I feared she was as much Michael's handiwork as my father's book. I would deal with that when the time came, however. Right now, it was time to see if Faron could pick up on my intentions.

"Perfect timing," I said to Cole and Rad.

"What do you need?" Cole asked.

"Bring Bane here. Without Faron."

He and Rad shared a look. Cole scratched his chin. "He's unlikely to leave her voluntarily."

"Do whatever it takes."

Cole nodded.

Rad stood firm. "Why?"

"I can't tell you yet. I need to know if she can read my mind and my intention for him while I'm inside this room." I pointed at Damon's phone. "We need everyone in the training center."

Without hesitation, he hit the intercom button. "Neve, make an announcement that all demons, angels, and support staff are to gather in the training center in ten minutes."

"Would you like assistance with this Bane character?" Dru asked Rad and Cole.

Cole waved him forward. "The more the merrier."

The three males filed out.

"What are you planning?" Damon asked.

I swept my fingers through the air, causing the door to close. "I'm beheading him."

Sal choked. "You're *what*? That's extreme, even for you. He's part human, is he not? A Nephilim?"

Nephilim, hmm. "I'm not sure what his makeup is or exactly what he's here for, but it doesn't matter. He's an unknown, and I suspect we'll get more out of Faron once he's out of the picture."

"Can you not put him in the dungeons?" the priest asked. "Why kill him?"

I had to stick to what I'd said I would do. The slightest waver would belie my true intent, and Faron might pick up on this test. "I'm unsure of his powers or who might show up to release him if I throw him down there. I can't take the chance. This is war, Sal. Concessions have to be made, even from you."

Frank backed toward the exit. "I don't want anything to do with all of this. I want to go home."

I motioned at one of the vampire guards, and he cut off Frank's escape.

"You know what I intend to do, which means you can't leave this room. No one leaves until I know if Faron can get through Vicky's ward."

"She can't," the witch insisted.

"We'll see," I uttered. I held up the book to Frank. "What does this say about helping me specifically?"

Pissed, he marched forward and ripped it from my grip. Flipping pages, he stopped and held a passage in front of my face. "Here, it says, and I quote, '*God's chief angel shall spear the Beast, and from their union a child shall be*—"

"Stop." I came off the desk, jerking the book away. The third vision Azaria had shown me flashed across my mind. I firmed my voice so it wouldn't shake. "How does spearing the Beast create a union?"

"Spear, in this case, refers to, um..." He shuffled his feet uncomfortably. "You know."

"His dick," Vicky supplied. "It's a euphemism. Michael and the Beast have sex and create a baby." The snark in her tone doubled. "Didn't anyone have the birds-and-the-bees talk with you, Kali?"

"Is this true?" Damon asked Frank, disbelief coloring his voice. "Michael and Kali..."

The door flew open. Dru materialized. He'd used his vampire speed to get back to us. "The male called Bane and the Fate he protects have disappeared. No one knows when they left or where they went."

I turned on Vicky. "It didn't work, Vicky. Try again."

She shot to her feet. "It did, too! They probably left before I even cast it."

Begrudgingly, I had to admit that was a possibility.

Dru fidgeted. "There's more. Cole believes the Fallen are up to something. A coup."

Salmad went white and eased around the vampire. "I shall go check."

Neve wheeled in, blocking his way. "There you are," she said to him. "Tabriss asked me to find you and give you a message. She says the timeline has been moved up, and she's enacting purgatory... purgation...purgato...? Something like that."

"*Purgatio*?" I barked. I didn't know Greek, but I knew enough Latin for the term to make my stomach flip. Purgatio meant 'purge.' The second vision was coming true. "From disciple to betrayer." I *tsked* and shook my head. "Here, I thought the most likely ones to go Judas on me were Tabriss or Frank. I guess I was fifty percent accurate. Salmad, I should have known."

His solemn expression turned hard and unforgiving. "My loyalty lies with the angels, not you."

"Sal?" Neve gave him a horrified look. "You betrayed Kali?"

Vicky cackled. Dru reached out and cold-cocked Sal. The priest's eyes rolled up in his head, and he dropped to the floor.

Damon grabbed his phone's handset and barked orders at whoever answered. "Lock it down, now. Yes, everything."

I raised a silent brow. Vicky dropped to the sofa cushion and began chanting again. Dru used magic to pull Neve into the room before shutting the door.

Damon hung up. "Protocol Obstruct engaged. Most of the Fallen were unaware of Tabriss accelerating the timeline of her plan, and Cole was able to restrain them in the training center. Those who were not captured are loose inside our walls, but they can't escape."

"You suspected her all along, didn't you?" I asked. "You sly archdemon! All that show about giving her more responsibility—you were just giving her rope to hang herself."

A hint of satisfaction flashed across his face. "The fight between good and evil has been going on for a long time, and I've been there for a good deal of it. You're not the only one who understands the imbalance of the situation we are in."

Nor was I the only one who understood battle strategy. I gave a partial bow to his calculating mind. "What about Lucifer and Amy?"

As if I had summoned them, the door, and whatever magic Dru had put on it, splintered. It fell into the room, a piece of it barely missing Neve and her wheelchair. She squeaked, and the vampire master snatched her out of harm's way before any damage was done.

Lucifer and Amy, with Azaria in her arms, marched inside. On their heels was Tabriss.

Lucifer Morningstar emitted enough raging power to blow back my hair. "What in the name of Heaven is going on?"

Without warning, Volante uncurled from my arm and morphed into sleek steel.

Angel steel.

A sword.

Michael's sword, to be precise.

Its blue flames licked the air. The wind died. Amy clutched the baby to her chest.

But Azaria's eyes were lit with the same blue light—a fire that blazed as they met mine.

In the next breath, the babe was in my arms, not Amy's. I shifted, juggling her chubby body and nearly dropping her. "Okay," I said as everyone gawked at me. "Didn't see that one coming."

24

*W*e added Rad to the packed room. As he raced in, he stopped short and, seeing me with Azaria and Michael's flaming sword, said, "What the fuck?"

My thought exactly.

Lucifer shot out a hand, and his angelic power reached for his daughter. I felt Azaria tug on my earth magic, and instantly, a shield formed in front of us, deflecting it.

"That wasn't me," I told him as his face went all kinds of shades of red. "She did that."

"Give her back," Amy demanded, holding out her hands. "Whatever you're doing, Kali, knock it off. This isn't funny."

"I'm not doing anything!" I could feel the baby sucking up more of my magic and funneling it into the shield. Not only mine—she was also using the sword's and Damon's. My tether to him gave her a channel to it. "Earlier, when I held her, I couldn't feel any magic in her. Now I know why. She's a siphon. Maybe an amplifier. Possibly both."

"A siphon?" Amy turned her alarmed face to Lucifer. "What's that?"

"I will roast you on a spit in the deepest gorge of Hell for eternity," Lucifer spat, "if you harm one hair on her head."

"I have no intention of harming her!" The sword handle warmed in my palm. Michael, you cunning, *porca miseria*. He'd tricked me. Tricked all of us. And it was no revelation what he expected me to do now that I held his sword and the babe.

Kill, the flames whispered.

"A siphon is exactly what it sounds like," Damon said. His archdemon was putting out some serious evil mojo. Our connection, however, was keeping me anchored, as it was supposed to, even with Azaria sucking on it. "She's extracting Kali's magic to use it for herself."

"Why?" Dru asked.

"Because she doesn't have her own yet," Frank said.

"But," I argued, "she must have powers of some sort."

He waggled a finger. "Not necessarily. If she can draw on the strongest magics that exist on this plane, she doesn't need her own."

I thought of the Lilith-Michael-possibly-Faron combo that Cole and I had encountered at the carnival grounds. "She can create her personal brand of magic by mixing that of others."

"She's a baby," Amy stated. "How would she even know how to do that or be able to handle it?"

"She's a powerhouse," Frank countered, "so she can manage and control immense amounts of power and direct it as she wills."

Rad narrowed his eyes at the girl. "Why use Kali's? Why not her father's?"

A damn good question. "Yeah, why me?" I asked.

Frank shifted, looking uncomfortable. "It would make sense for her to be drawn to the most potent magic available."

I chanced a peek at Lucifer's grim face, masking any surprise or troubling emotions that revelation brought. If he wouldn't ask the question, then I would. "How is it possible that I have more potent magic than an archangel?"

Frank scratched the back of his head. "Correct me if I'm wrong, but you are bloodbonded to one. You're also a *vitium* halfbreed who's shared blood with a master vampire."

"Your heritage contributes as well," Lucifer added. "Your ties to Mary Magdalene and Jesus create even more supremacy."

Dru gave me an appraising smile—the bastard was enjoying this. Sal groaned and pushed himself up to a sitting position. Frank dropped to the couch next to Vicky, sweating like we were already in the fires of Hell.

Rad looked shell-shocked. Neve murmured prayers under her breath, holding onto her crucifix pendant for dear life.

Behind me, Damon prowled the edges of the shield, attempting to communicate through our channel. Only intermittent words came through. *How...I...help?*

How could he help? Hell, if I knew. "Everybody, take a deep breath. I'm not going to hurt the child."

"Return her to us immediately," Lucifer ordered.

I glanced down at Azaria. She was chewing on one of her

fists. "You need to go see your mom and dad now." I moved toward them, but her body went rigid, and the shield blocked me. I glanced at Amy and Lucifer. "She won't let me near you."

Amy wrung her hands. "Azaria? What's wrong? Why are you doing this?"

The girl lifted her gaze to mine, the blue fire blazing in her irises. Did she not realize she was in danger from me and the sword?

Her sticky hand reached out and tapped my cheek. She gurgled, and my mind went blank—until she filled it with another vision.

I felt a quickening in my lower belly—a quickening I'd never experienced before. Didn't matter—I had no doubt what it signified.

"No," I said through gritted teeth. "No, no, no, no."

But the vision continued to play out, leaving me frozen and stupefied. I tore my eyes from her gaze, meeting Rad's.

He looked as sick as I felt, but when our eyes met, he covered his horror and gave me a reassuring nod.

The matrix.

How do we break free?

By killing the girl? The one chance that humanity had of surviving the wages of sin?

Her tiny nails dug into my cheek, forcing my attention back to her. This time, in her gaze, I saw the future of the world—the first vision—play out again, but from a different perspective.

In it, I knelt on the scorched, barren earth. Lucifer held her limp body and the flaming sword, his intent to strike me clear. As my view swung in an arc, however, I saw who was behind me, guarding the gates of Paradise.

Michael.

He would never allow Lucifer to enter. Would not save humanity. Azaria pushed the truth into my mind.

Every single entity on earth was steeped in sin. If she united Heaven and Earth...

All would cease to exist.

All.

I gasped. *Every entity*—demon, human, Fallen.

Except for me and Lucifer.

Even she would die.

Why me? I asked. *Why would I survive?*

My belly pinched again.

Oh, hell no. I would not allow myself to be Michael's baby mama.

The sword flared bright, and she switched the vision.

Michael and I were repopulating the globe with his children.

A New Earth.

I'm a demon, I insisted in a panic. *He would never use me for that purpose. I'm full of sin.*

She gurgled and grinned. *He will save you. This is your destiny.*

Damon's voice forced its way past her shield. *Sacrifice... yourself.*

What did that mean? Give myself to the archangel? No way.

Sacrifice. Understanding nudged my brain.

I tore my eyes from Azaria and raised the sword.

But there was no way I could plunge it into myself when the girl laid her head on my chest, clinging to me to stop my plan.

Those in the room gasped, thinking I was about to spear her, and several magics hit me at once—Lucifer's, Amy's, Rad's, and Damon's.

Azaria and her shield sucked all of it up, her body going rigid in my hold. A cacophony of sound exploded in my skull, and I cried out, dropping to my knees. I released the sword, but it refused to fall, and she placed her hands on my temples. A new plan—hers—forced its way into my brain.

She was ordering me to save her family.

My legs obeyed of their own accord, and I rose to my feet. "The child controls me," I said to the others, who had surged around us when I fell but were still unable to touch us. "She has a message and a strategy for what we're going to do."

"Tell us," Damon demanded.

I looked at Lucifer. "There's something I need to show you first. *We* need to show you."

The archangel wasn't used to being ordered around, being denied anything, or feeling a lack of control. I understood the emotions that flickered across his face and the fear that burned in his eyes. "Do it," he growled.

"Don't try to take her from me. If you do, she'll resist."

He nodded and stepped forward. Azaria allowed him to pass through her shield and join us inside the bubble.

She reached out a hand, and he kissed it so tenderly that it made my heart clench. He bowed slightly so she could slide it to his temple, and I closed my eyes as the scorched earth vision filled both of our minds. When it was done playing out, he drew back, frowning at me. "Why would you do that?"

"*Me*? You're the one who's going to burn it all to a crisp after Azaria..." I knew better than to say it out loud and panic Amy more than she already was. "After the merge doesn't work and Paradise is not restored."

"If I do it, why would you still be alive and not...?" He stopped himself, and we both glanced at the baby.

"Because of Michael. For whatever reason, he's chosen me to help him"—I glanced at Rad and back to Lucifer, wincing at what I had to say—"repopulate the earth with his offspring."

Rad turned livid green. "*What*?"

"It's not going to happen," I assured him. "Azaria and I are on the same page. It sucks, but we're not going to allow Paradise to return. If we do, there will be no humans, or anyone else, to enjoy it."

Confusion flooded the room. "I don't understand," Amy shouted over the others. "What is this vision she's showing you?"

In the distance, we heard muffled screaming. "I wish I could explain," I told her, "but we don't have time. We have an uprising to put down." I looked Lucifer square in the eye, knowing he wanted to burn me to a crisp right then and there, and it was only his daughter who kept him from doing so. "What you decide to do right now decides whether your family lives or dies. We either trust each other and stop Michael's plans for good, or that vision you saw will play out. Choose carefully."

There was a long pause, the background yelling and shouting growing closer and more intense.

He wasn't one to be hurried, though. Even those in the room became agitated at his delayed response.

Something hit the wall outside, and I felt Damon's magic put a barrier across the door so no one could enter.

Azaria kicked her feet against my body, staring at her father over her shoulder. The sword flared brighter, as did her eyes, flames shooting out toward him.

His black irises went blue, and I realized their communication was not only her sharing her intention but also demanding his acquiescence.

Not to save the world.

Not to save the Fallen.

To save the three of them.

Their family, who would be stuck on Earth forever and could never return to Heaven.

But they'd be alive and together.

The flames winked out of his eyes. A muscle ticked in his jaw. Nothing meant more to him than Amy and Azaria. The only way to save them was to call off his war. To concede to his brother, whom he had been fighting for eternity.

Azaria flopped against me, resting her head on my chest. I sensed her tuning into my heartbeat, her tiny human body tired. She sucked a thumb into her mouth and closed her eyes.

Lucifer raised his hands in frustration. "Why would Tabriss and the other Fallen rise against me?"

"Because Michael has convinced her to recruit them to his side. She wants nothing more than to return to Heaven to be with him, and that's probably what he's promised her if she does this. She doesn't just plan to stop you—she plans to obliterate you."

His jaw ticked again. "The only way to do that is with the sword you hold."

"She thinks she can take it from me."

The room vibrated with his anger. "Let's go show her she's wrong."

25

*U*nfortunately, she wasn't.

When Lucifer and I materialized in front of her, holding court in the training center, Tabriss only smiled, glancing at the sword in my hand. "Took you long enough."

Before he'd transported us here, I'd handed out assignments to each of those in Damon's office. Everyone had something to do before they met us here to back me up.

My main job was to protect the girl, although I sensed Azaria could do that on her own as long as she could draw on my power. I hefted her on my hip, allowing the magic in the blade to reach for Tabriss and tease her. Her followers drew closer to her, filling the gym with their power and something else.

Malice.

My magic tasted it, and the peppery flavor left a bitter taste on my tongue. Tabriss wanted the sword to eliminate me and Lucifer, and she planned to take Heaven for herself.

Greedy bitch.

Still, I had to admire her ambition, even if her methods were less than admirable for someone of her standing. Was it any different than me wanting to be queen of Hell?

My motives were not about power or revenge, though. I wanted to safeguard those I cared about, and the only way I could do that was to be in charge.

Lucifer spoke before I could. "Michael has deranged your thinking. You are a powerful being, but even with your meager supporters, you will fail."

"Michael has clarified things for me." She took a step toward me, holding out a hand. "Give me the sword."

She assumed my bloodbond with him would force me to do her bidding. He'd no doubt claimed I couldn't resist, and he had pre-programmed the weapon to respond to her. I acted as if it was tugging away from me.

The grief over losing Volante soared inside me all over again. I had already become accustomed to the whip being back in my life, and now it was as if she had been obliterated a second time.

Clever on Michael's part to use something I loved against me. He would do the same with all those I cared for—Rad, Damon, Cole, Neve, Di, Maddy...all of them. Even Dru.

Do the unexpected. I was certainly trying. Keeping my enemies off guard was more fun than going at them head-on since most beings—human, demon, or otherwise—tended to dig in their heels when challenged.

Willingly turning the blade over to her was a solid no, but making her think I was on her side would keep her from raising her defenses. "Before I do that," I said, tightening my grip and thrusting the sharp point into the ground, "I want to cut a deal."

Lucifer had the good sense to look shocked. Tabriss dropped her hand and shot me a vexed glare. "No deals. The sword is mine." Her hard eyes flicked to Lucifer and back to me, only now seeming to take in the fact I carried his daughter. "You've served your purpose, demon. Hand it over, and I'll spare your life."

"Yeah, about that…" The room filled with earth magic as demons began filing in from the entrances and materializing through the walls, floor, and ceiling.

Phew. Vicky had come through.

Next to me, the current queen of Hell shimmered into view, her evil energy adding a thick layer to Azaria's shield. "Tabriss," Lilith purred in her sultry voice. "We finally meet." She sniffed the air, drawing it into her lungs and making a soft mewing sound like the angel's magic was the best thing she'd sampled in a long time. Maybe ever. "Yes, you'll do fine. The taste of your blood will be…exquisite on my tongue."

"What is she…?" The color drained from Tabriss's face. "What have you done?" she snarled at me. She knew exactly what I'd done—it was written all over her face. "You'll pay for this."

Vicky rushed in, falling at Lilith's feet. "My queen." She bowed her head and kissed the demon mother's hand. "I've waited so long."

Lilith peered at me, brows rising in question. I nodded. "Lilith, may I present your most ardent fan—Victoria DeClement. Head of the *Satina Arcanum.*"

Lilith touched the top of her head. "Witch and vampire, hmm. An interesting combination."

Especially since the two species didn't mix or play well

together. "A potent hybrid," I added. *Please take her off my hands.* "An asset to your plans."

Lucifer ground his teeth so hard I could hear it.

"No," Tabriss yelled. "You cannot walk on sacred ground! Where angels stand!"

Lilith flicked her gaze to her, back to me. "You haven't told her?"

"We were getting to it."

"Please take me away from here," Vicky begged. "I wish to serve you and only you."

Yes, please do. "You can see how powerful she is, my queen," I said.

"Enough!" Tabriss screamed. "Take your demons and leave now!"

"Leave? Why would she do that?" I grinned. "The party is just getting started."

Due to the fact Tabriss was my blood slave, I let my magic snap at her like a snarling dog. It demanded her loyalty and obedience—yet she had been working on ways around that. I suspected Salmad had been assisting her with breaking our connection.

Kirill and Yasmine appeared, their archdemon energies filling the space. They were followed by the other *vitiums*—including Sal. He looked as pale and shocked as Tabriss did and tried to catch her eye as if to apologize as Seraphina, Akimo, and Shayne circled the Fallen.

Damon walked beside Sal, his magic forcing him to stand against her. Otherwise, the mad priest would have joined her ranks.

Idiot.

A second layer of demons—Cole and his Merc soldiers —added a barrier to our flanks.

Lilith drew Vicky off her knees and placed her in a position of honor slightly behind her on her left. "You are outnumbered," she said to Tabriss. "What are you going to do?"

"Michael and the forces of Heaven are on my side," Tabriss insisted, her voice echoing in the gym. "Righteousness is on *my side*."

The Fallen around her murmured encouragement. However, the way their eyes skittered about, taking in the army I had gathered to shut this down, gave them away. They knew that even with their power, they were sitting ducks.

Several of Lilith's minions—mouth breathers, oozing pus from various orifices, and sporting too many eyes—raked barbed tails along the ground as they paced closer and closer to the angels. As if fearing their touch might contaminate them, the angels scooted and jostled each other, knocking into their fellow Fallen, disgust evident on their faces.

I raised the sword. "Back down, swear allegiance to Lucifer, and I'll give you this."

Again, I'd surprised him. He didn't react outwardly at my command to Tabriss, but his energy was all over the place. It was unusual for him, but then again, Azaria had upset his world in many ways. His love for her had shaken his standard control and absolute dominance and turned him into putty in her hands. He was off-balance, desiring nothing more than to protect her at all costs.

So...rather than forcing Tabriss and her followers to

swear allegiance to me, which was what Lucifer expected, I'd turned the tables. She'd become too much of a constant burr under my ass, anyway, and I was sick of her. Like Vicky, I was hoping to unload her on someone else.

Tabriss sneered. "Why would I do that?"

"Because you want to live. If you attempt to harm any of us, Azaria will raze the entire earth." I tilted my head at the sleeping child. "I've seen it—what she can do. If the prophecy is fulfilled, we'll get the same outcome. Which happens to be exactly what Michael wants. To wipe the earth of all humans, demons, and you, the Fallen."

A collective gasp went up. Hunh. They didn't know. Even Lilith turned that querying expression on me.

Rad entered with Dru, the two of them hauling Frank with them. Di, Maddy, and Neve followed on their heels. Di carried the dog.

Tabriss raised her voice another octave. "You're lying. Michael loves me." She pounded a fist against her chest. "He will welcome me and those who follow me into Heaven. We are his chosen!"

A murmur of ascent. Angel power thrummed, their bodies beginning to glow with it.

"So long as you prove your loyalty," I countered. "That doesn't sound like love to me—that sounds like manipulation. Plus, it's a lie. He has no intention of allowing anyone touched by sin to enter his kingdom. That includes every single one of you." I pulled the sword out of the floor and flashed it at her, its fake yet still beautiful flames flaring higher thanks to Lucifer. "By the way, another tidbit you might not have figured out yet—he's making plans to repopulate the Earth with his own creations." I lowered the sword and let the demon in me shine through my eyes. "Guess who he's chosen to make those babies with?"

Deathly silence descended. Tabriss opened her mouth to retort but snapped it shut. She wanted to believe I was lying, that I was tricking her somehow, but she could see the truth in my black demon eyes.

"Never," she sneered. "You are evil. You are one of the vices."

"I know, right? What is he thinking?" I propped the sword against my leg and patted my lower belly. "Makes no sense to me, either, but I've already got one in the oven."

A breeze kicked up. I couldn't look Rad in the eye. I knew it was all he could do to hold back his chaos from breaking free. I was actually counting on that helping us when the fight broke out.

Because there *would* be a fight.

"I hate you." The words came out soft but full of venom. "I'm going to kill you."

"You're going to try," I corrected. "Good luck with that."

"She's telling the truth," Frank yelled from between Cole and Rad. "I've seen the prophecies. Everyone touched by sin will be annihilated. That means us, the Fallen."

Tabriss turned on him, clearing a path of followers as she marched up to him. "You're lying because you're on her side."

He stood his ground, which surprised me. "I'm not. Ask Sal. He'll confirm what I read."

She whipped her head to the priest. "Is this true?"

It gutted him to nod. He loved her—I could see it in every breath he took. "I'm sorry."

With perfect timing, Amy and her companions,

including Gabriel, arrived. "I'm not," she said. "You crossed the wrong witch."

"Michael!" Tabriss screamed. "I need you!"

But there was no reply from her heavenly boyfriend. "I warded the Institute," Vicky said, flashing her fangs. "He can't hear you."

A momentary pause reigned. Then Tabriss vanished, only to materialize a few feet in front of me. "The sword," she commanded in her divine voice. It vibrated through the space, shaking the rafters. "Give me the sword."

Azaria awoke, and the shield intensified. "It won't make any difference," I told her, her magic ripping into me like razor blades. "It won't save you."

"Maybe not," she growled, "but it will kill you."

She tore through Azaria's defensive barrier as if it were nothing.

And grabbed the sword.

26

*S*he wrenched the sword from my hand. Thank goodness Azaria was playing her part, lowering her shield enough for the angel to do so. I wanted to kiss the top of the girl's head but didn't want to give away our next play.

Tabriss stepped back, pointing the tip at my heart—right where Azaria clung to me. A collective gasp went up from those gathered. Even the most hardened member of the Kali squad would never point Michael's sword at the Chosen Child.

Of course, we were surrounded by low-level demons who would like nothing better than to watch an angel skewer the girl. They'd be happy to join in, taking me out with her.

Lilith had a firm leash on all of them. She chuckled at the shock-filled faces of Tabriss's followers. Most of them hadn't realized the extremes their leader would go to to get her way.

Which side would they choose now? Would they continue to follow her, or would they reconsider their stand?

"Michael told me you would do this," Tabriss hissed, her grip tightening on the handle. "That you would lie and scheme and say anything you could to make me doubt him."

"He's the one keeping you out of Heaven," I told her. "It's not God. I've seen Michael at the gates, guarding them." I turned Azaria and held her up. Her feet kicked in the air, and she gurgled with happy anticipation. The shield she'd kept around us was totally gone. "This child is a siphon and an amplifier. She has no innate power but can draw it from Michael to unlock those gates." I lowered her and handed her to her mother. Amy hugged her tight, giving a small whimper of relief.

"None of that matters," I continued. "Each and every one of you has been tainted by sin and cannot cross that threshold. You can stay here on Earth and live on, though. You can do good and help humans turn their lives around."

The Fallen turned to each other, murmuring. Some shook their heads, while others nodded. It took several heartbeats before Lilith caught on to my plan. "*Help* humans? You promised my demons would have freedom here to feast on them."

I lowered my voice so only she could hear. "This is all a ploy, remember? Your demons will get first crack at the angels, then the humans."

Skepticism colored her features, but she nodded.

I'd left Vicky out of this part of the plan so she didn't contradict me. She still didn't trust me, however, and wasn't as gullible as Lilith. She stayed close to her evil mentor. "I'll make sure she doesn't double-cross you," she told Lilith.

So many deceptions. They were beginning to overlap too much. I needed to wrap this up quickly before I had a massacre on my hands.

"No," Tabriss called out. Her hand shook from the sword's weight and what she was about to do. "We are going home, but before we do, we are obliterating you."

"I came from you," I reminded her. "I took on your pride when Jesus cast the vices out of you. I was the one to find you and save you from Big Mo. I brought you here to remind you of who you are and what you can do. This is how you repay me?"

The memories flickered behind her eyes, but she squashed them. "Regardless, you're evil. It's my duty to exterminate you."

Like I was a bug.

I spread my arms wide, leaving my chest vulnerable. "Give it the old college try, then."

She lunged. The tip of the sword tore through my clothes and nipped my skin before Lilith was there, knocking the weapon from Tabriss's hand. As if a flag had been thrown, the hoard of demons descended on the angels, the battle breaking out around us.

Vicky shoved me aside to get to Tabriss as Lilith swiped her claws at the angel's face. Tabriss fled back several steps, dropping the sword.

A surge from behind her shoved her into me, and the two of us went down, her on top. She scrambled away on all fours, snatching up the sword, and dematerialized.

"Kali!"

I gained my feet to see Cole racing toward me with the true sword of Michael's in hand. He tossed it through the air, and I caught it as the melee around us intensified. Angelic magic lit the space with a nearly blinding light. Demonic magic rushed up from beneath my feet, fiery and hungry, as screams echoed in the high-ceilinged room.

"Where did she go?" I yelled to Lucifer. He was hustling Amy and the baby toward an exit. He threw a glance back at me and pointed up.

I caught Damon's eye. "The roof!"

He nodded, blocking one of the angels. "Go."

I started for the same exit Lucifer and Amy were disappearing through, but the sword flared a bright blue, and the world went upside down.

I fell to my hands and knees, gasping, the blade clinking on the floor. The room around me morphed into a black nothingness, and I was floating in it, staring toward a central, darker point in the far distance.

Having lived in Chicago for decades, I knew the sensation of winter—freezing temperatures, stinging ice, numbing snow. The cold that hit me was much more brutal than anything I'd ever experienced. It froze my lungs. My heart stalled out. My organs turned to ice cubes, my bones to icicles.

Everywhere I looked, there was nothing but darkness.

The Unknowing

A thought, there and then gone.

I was blind, naked, exposed to that encroaching darkness. To that void.

Not a void. *Devoid.*

Barren. Vacant. Bereft.

Something powerful existed beyond it, but I couldn't see it or reach it.

Was it...God?

The point in the distance began to shimmer. I could only watch as it became a portal, yawning open like a giant mouth that would consume everything, including me. Instead, it began spitting things out, like the ground at the carnival vomiting out beetles.

Galaxies, stars, and a cosmos were expelled from the gaping maw. I was caught in the maelstrom, seized by unseen forces, and then blown apart.

My vision whited out. All sensation ceased.

I ceased.

I became the darkness. The cold. The nothingness.

I was undone. *Unknown.*

As if I'd never existed.

The silence and oblivion called to my soul, offering peace.

A false promise, a trick to tempt me into giving up.

There was something still there—a spark. A twinge.

My magic and something else.

Knowingness.

I would not go into that unknown, become nothing. Not without a fight.

I clawed for that spark and snagged it with a talon of magic. Ripping into the darkness, I rent it apart. I screamed, even though there was no sound.

Grabbing hold, I twisted and jerked, mutilated the piece I'd snagged. I took it into my body and absorbed it with my magic.

I spit it back out.

Planets, quasars, meteorites... I devoured them, feeding myself and giving myself form and structure again.

I heaved a breath.

I stared at the all-consuming darkness that loomed.

The darkness—the Unknowing—stared back.

I won't give up, I told it.

The Unknowing blinked.

A child's giggle filtered through the devoid, barren thing that watched me. I felt that twinge again.

That spark.

Michael's essence.

My vision whited out like before, and I was dumped—expelled—onto the roof of the Institute. I somersaulted ass over tea cart.

Tabriss stared up at the heavens, her voice pleading as she cried, "Where are you? Why have you forsaken me?"

The fake sword that Lucifer and Vicky had bespelled to act like Michael's lay tossed aside. The sky frowned down on her with violent, boiling clouds. Thunder boomed, shaking the building. Flashes of lightning lit the lake, where the water climbed in savage waves. Waterspouts formed.

"He hasn't forsaken you," I shouted over the noise. The knowingness circled through my system, revealing a truth I couldn't doubt. "Michael did all of this to save you."

Her head whirled in my direction. "What?"

"He never intended to let you die."

Her chest heaved. "But I want to go to Heaven. I hate it here."

"You can't, Tabriss. None of the Fallen can, and I think, deep down, you know that. Trying to restore Paradise is a pipe dream and will only lead to the destruction of everything. Build a new world here. With me. With us."

She shook her head, frantic. Wind whipped her hair into

a halo. "I hate you as much as I hate this place! You've ruined everything."

"Michael wanted me to sabotage Lucifer and the Fallen to save you. Do you get that? If I failed, he had you primed to be the one to do it. Or Lilith. Or... Anyone, really. As long as he could stop the prophecy from coming true. He played us all, not because of a desire for power but because he still loves you, Tabriss. He knew that allowing the prophecy to be fulfilled would obliterate you."

She stomped toward me, furious. Her hands were fists, and she was ready to swing. "You're lying!"

I came to my feet and balled my fists, also ready for a showdown. "I'm telling you that the love of your life, your soulmate, is trying to save you, and you accuse me of lying?"

It seemed so ingrained in her—not trusting me—that she couldn't wrap her head around the fact. "This is a trick. You're trying to stop me from reuniting with him."

"It's no trick. Trust me, if I could get rid of you, I would." The storm intensified, rain sheeting down on us in such a torrential wave that it nearly drove me backward. I had to raise my voice even louder. "You may not be able to enter Heaven, but he can visit Earth and be with you. Like Lucifer and Amy. Keisha and Gabriel."

"You said he wanted to create a New Earth with his children. That he picked you to be his mate."

I sluiced water off my face. "A clever misdirection to plant his essence inside of me, causing me to believe he had impregnated me with a child. That wasn't it." The Unknowing—be it God or something else—had come for me. Had tried to delete my existence. Why, I wasn't sure, but I must have posed a threat to it. Still posed a threat.

Michael had saved me.

Would wonders never cease?

How had he known I would need his essence to survive?

I wasn't sure it mattered. I was different now. I'd taken a piece of the Unknowing into myself. I knew things I shouldn't.

And I would never *unknow* them.

Damon, Lucifer, Rad, and Frank crashed through the roof door, spilling onto the flat expanse. "Stand down," Damon ordered Tabriss in his archdemon voice.

Rad's glare turned shocked when he looked at me. "What happened to you?"

I glanced down at myself, but all I saw were wet clothes and dirty boots. "Weird story. I'll catch you up later."

Tabriss's wild eyes darted from me to them and back. "I will never stop fighting for what's mine!"

Lucifer waved the rea flaming sword of Michael. "What's *yours*? None of this is yours, Tabriss. None of it. I offered you what you've been missing since Jesus left Mary Magdalene and turned you into a walking disaster. You've thrown it all back at me."

Her pleading gaze turned skyward once more. "Please, Michael. Help me!"

Lightning flashed in the distance. She moved toward the edge of the roof. I skirted past one of the HVAC systems, glancing at Rad, his face grim. The wind roared past my head, lifting my drenched hair.

"He's already helped you," I insisted to Tabriss. "He's done exactly what he could to keep you from extinction."

"Stay away from me," she screamed. "You'll say anything to make me believe you're his chosen mate."

"Aren't you listening? I don't *want* to be his mate, and believe me, he has no designs on me." I glanced at Rad again, my true soulmate. "Michael planted a seed of his essence inside me to keep me from being blotted out by a force greater than all of us. The Unknowing tried to claim me. Tried to remove me from this world." The archangel's reason for saving me was unclear, but it seemed that if The Unknowing had succeeded, it must have presented a dire outcome. One Michael wanted to avoid. "There's no baby, Tabriss. No connection or relationship between me and him other than a very healthy dislike."

She struck out with her angel magic. After my trip through the darkness, I hadn't restored my protective shields. Her power flared as bright as the blue flames licking the blade and knocked me on my ass.

I skidded across the wet asphalt roof, and before I could stand, she snatched up the discarded sword and bore down on me with a speed I hadn't anticipated.

The others shouted my name, and I felt the impact of all of their magics lash out at her, but she had fully come into her divine mojo and managed to get close enough to drive the blade into my chest.

The world slowed to a crawl, and my demon revolted against the cleaving of my heart. Shock rendered me immobile.

She thrust it deeper, letting out a cry of rage and triumph.

"I tried," I yelled at Michael. He was listening, that much I knew. "I'm done saving your precious pet."

She saw the demon take over when my eyes turned black

and jumped back, releasing her grip on the sword. "Why won't you die?"

Sacrifice yourself. Damon's words rang in my head, even as my heart clanged hard against the steel. Still unsure of the meaning, everything in me rebelled against the idea.

My hand shot out, grabbing her by the throat and squeezing. "Do you know what the most destructive force on Earth is?" She couldn't answer, her nails scratching at my arm frantically, her fingers trying to pry mine from her windpipe. "Vengeance," I spit. "The motivation for revenge is anger, but it's ultimately powered by satisfaction and enjoyment. Let me be clear,"—I applied even more pressure—"I'm going to enjoy this."

Knowing I was about to end what she believed to be her immortal life, she hit me with her angelic power again, but my demon was in full force. It bounced back on her. She grabbed the sword's handle and tried to wrench it free, then drive it deeper. Our close proximity stopped her. The sawing action created immense pressure inside me, but I didn't release my hold.

Her wings, which I'd never seen, unfolded with a snap. Enormous, with an expanse that covered ten feet or more, they rose like a hawk preparing to dive. To kill.

From out of the clouds, Michael descended, his wings on full display. The storm ceased. "Release her," he commanded of me.

"Fat chance." I curled my lips back and growled.

Then I snapped her neck.

27

*M*ultiple things happened at that point.

Tabriss exploded in a brilliant light show, turning every drop of rain into a rainbow. The clouds overhead parted, and a clear night sky became visible.

I fell to my knees, the blade bobbing, still embedded in my chest. Rad raced to me.

Tabriss was an angel—she couldn't be killed by anything less than a blade designed to do so—Michael's, in fact. She shouldn't have disintegrated like that. Had I actually destroyed her?

Before Rad touched me, there was a pop, and I went spiraling, landing in the exact same position on sandy terrain.

A glance showed me I was in the Lost City of Angels.

And I wasn't alone.

Michael paced at one end of the expanse, a set of tall, pearly gates behind him. Lucifer stood rigidly at the other end, holding a flaming sword.

It was so much like Azaria's vision I sucked in a breath.

Hadn't I aborted the prophecy? What would happen now?

Azaria wasn't in sight, and as her father stalked to me, I lifted my chin rather than bowing my head.

I wasn't dying today.

Maybe not ever.

Something different coursed through my blood and bones. Whatever it was, it was immortal.

I'd destroyed an angel because of it.

Lucifer didn't attempt to behead me, which was somewhat of a relief. He yanked the weapon from my chest. No blood emerged, and my heart chugged hard once, twice, three times, before resuming its normal rhythm.

"Thanks," I said on a ragged breath. "What are we doing here?"

He faced his brother, who continued to pace in front of the gates. "I suspect we are about to find out."

We trudged toward Michael, the sand rippling under our feet. It made me feel drunk. Gusts of wind blew in one direction and then the other, adding to the sensation. Michael only glanced at his sword, avoiding our eyes. "Big surprise," he snarled. "You've ruined my plans again, Kali Sweet."

The closer we got to the gates, the taller they became. "I'm not sorry about Tabriss." I wasn't sure I'd obliterated her, but it seemed so. I stopped a few yards back from him and the gates. The glow and power they emitted made my skin crawl. "And I'm not sorry about screwing up the prophecy."

"The prophecy was false, and you know it."

"Which one? The original about Azaria, or the one about you and the Beast?"

He dismissed both with a flippant wave. "You figured out that I tampered with your father's writings. Your mother predicted no such thing concerning how we would stop the original prophecy."

"Why did you do it?"

He stopped pacing, his expression stern and unrelenting when he turned it on me. In it, I could see a resemblance to Lucifer—one I'd never noticed before. "I thought you had it all figured out. Isn't that what you told Tabriss?"

"You could've simply sat down with me and explained it."

"No, he couldn't," Lucifer said. "Neither you nor I would have believed him, even if he'd tried."

Michael tapped the end of his nose. "What fun would that be? This way, Kali gets to be a hero again. You do love playing the hero, don't you, demon?"

"Fuck you. You led all of us on a wild goose chase, knowing this whole time that if the prophecy came true, it would annihilate everyone tainted by sin." The adrenaline was wearing off, and my limbs felt shaky. "Talk about burying the lead."

"I didn't know that until a few hours ago," he countered. "I was trying to save Heaven from being overrun by tainted angels, yes. We call them Fallen for a reason. They don't belong here," he gestured behind him.

"Explain," Lucifer demanded.

"Let's say, from the mouths of babes—one in particular —come all kinds of interesting information." When Lucifer stiffened, realizing Michael was suggesting Azaria had told him, he made that dismissive gesture again. "You may not like it, brother, but my tie to her exists for a reason. She showed me what would happen if you succeeded with your plans and..."

When he didn't finish, the third and final vision she'd shown me snapped into place. It hadn't made sense before. Now, considering what lay behind those gates, it did. "They're all gone, aren't they?"

His brows bunched. "You know?"

"She showed me."

"Who?" Lucifer asked. "Who's gone?"

Michael's voice dropped. "The human souls who are supposed to be in there." He pointed. "All those who repented while still on Earth and were supposed to receive their reward when they died...they're gone."

A strained silence hung in the air as Lucifer and I took it in. "But, where are they?" I asked.

"Hell," Lucifer supplied. "Is that what you're telling us? That they weren't saved?"

Michael pointed at the gates. "There are many levels here, and I swear, I've checked every one of them. All the previous souls that were inside—millions of them—are now gone."

I blinked several times, trying to imagine where they might be. Surely, Lucifer was wrong. "Who would force them out? Are we sure they're in Hell?"

"I had Lilith check," Michael told us. "They aren't there, either. They aren't anywhere. They've just disappeared."

That's why he'd formed a partnership with her—he couldn't enter the Pit on his own. "To get Lilith to check for you, you had to agree to help her with her plan to take over the Earth."

He nodded.

Lucifer shook his head. "It's not possible. Souls don't simply cease to exist."

I searched for a solution. "Could they have all been reincarnated?"

Michael raked his hands over his face and into his hair. "If they had, the planet's population would have doubled overnight. I don't know where they went, and I believe other beings are disappearing, too. That's the reason I brought the principalities here and put them on ice. I'm protecting them."

"From what?" Lucifer asked.

"That's what I've been trying to figure out."

I glanced around, not seeing the monoliths of ice. "They're here?" I asked. "Where?"

He motioned to his right. "Around the corner. Simply a different part of this dimension."

"Why didn't you tell me?" Lucifer questioned. "Why didn't you tell the others?"

"What I've uncovered... I couldn't trust anyone with it. Not even our brothers and sisters."

"Until now," I said. "Azaria has assured you that we're trustworthy."

He snorted. "Trustworthy? No. But, apparently, you two are my only hope at stopping the annihilation of everything."

The blue sword flamed brighter, confirming what he said. Lucifer and I exchanged a weighted glance.

Michael went on, "The Omnis—ever heard of them?"

The word buzzed in my brain. "The qualities of God? Omniscience, omnipotence?"

"Not exactly," he replied. "The Omnis are entities beyond..." He looked flustered, then gestured at the space around us. "Beyond all of this. There are four. What we call God, Our Father, is but one of them. They're an unknowing force, something exceeding even an angel's comprehension. Timeless, immortal, all-being." He produced what looked like my father's book and tossed it to me. "That's the original, I swear. I didn't tamper with it. It claims The Omnis are the origins of all supernaturals that exist."

"Even us?" Lucifer asked.

Michael nodded. "Even us, brother."

An *unknowing* force, something beyond even an angel's comprehension. "I've met one of them," I blurted.

"I thought so." Michael looked me over from head to toe. "He's clever, undermining you and the others."

He? "Wait...who are you talking about?"

His face turned skeptical. "Who are *you* talking about?"

"Not a who. A...thing. An entity. In the training center, the sword showed me a place—another plane, I think. It was darker than anything I've ever experienced and so cold. Totally devoid of anything but a presence. It *looked* at me and..." I shuddered. "And then, it tried to obliterate me. Not just kill me, but wipe me out of existence. As if I'd never been created."

Both angels stared at me with such intensity that my demon came to attention, ready to defend and protect me, ready to attack.

"You saw it?" Lucifer said. "This thing."

"I fought it. I had to. I ripped into it and absorbed some

of its...essence. I sort of ate it." I glanced at Michael. "I thought you knew I would have to do that, and that's why you gave me your spark. So I would win."

He shook his head. "I gave you that spark so you could defeat Lilith when the time came."

Oh. That changed a few things. I glanced down at myself. "Well, now there's a piece of it in me, along with your angel essence."

They both stepped back.

It would have been funny, except it wasn't. If knowing I had even a smidge of these Omni-thingies inside me made two of the most powerful beings in this universe back away? I didn't want to think what that meant.

The realization of what they might do to me hit next. Why had I opened my mouth? I should have kept this a secret until I understood the consequences.

I wasn't about to let them imprison me here or anywhere else.

Lucifer examined the sword. "Is it possible that The Omnis consumed the souls that were in Heaven?"

The fire rippled—another confirmation?

"Those things are *here*?" I asked. "They can access Heaven?"

"I believe so," Michael said. "The text claims that our Creator stole fragments from each and turned them into artifacts." He continued to eye me with a healthy dose of wariness. "He hid the artifacts on Earth and then covered the Earth with humans. Since The Omnis' MO is chaos and destruction, I believe they walk among humans right now, searching for those artifacts. They need to be whole to create their own dimensions, and they are consuming souls to keep up their energy."

The ramifications were staggering. "We need to find those artifacts before they do," I said.

"And stop them from feasting on souls," Lucifer added.

"How?" Michael began pacing again. "I've been over and over it, and I can't figure out where the artifacts are or how to retrieve them. I've searched every ancient text and questioned every immortal that I know. Outside of what's in that book"—he pointed to the volume in my hand—"nothing is recorded about them. How do we fight an enemy we don't know?"

Lucifer's scrutiny zeroed in on me. "If you have a piece of one inside you, you're connected to them. We can use that to find the artifacts and destroy them."

The sword flared again.

I gripped my father's book. "Destroy them? Don't we want to give the artifacts back so they'll leave?"

Michael stopped pacing and hung his head. "If they become whole again, they will wipe all of us out." He gazed at me from beneath his lowered brows. "Just like the one you met tried to do to you. Not simply kill you but erase your very existence throughout all time and space. All souls. All planets, stars, and dimensions. They'll wipe the deck with us."

I didn't need the sword to tell me this was the truth. 'Wiping the deck' with those who got out of line was my specialty. "As an act of revenge."

"Can you feel it?" Lucifer asked. "Whatever that essence is inside you, can you tap into it?"

I wasn't sure I wanted to. "I was just impaled with a

sword through my heart after encountering an unknowable, immortal *thing*. I'm not even sure I can conjure my magic at the moment, much less use an alien one to scry for artifacts."

The blade's light banked, showing my lie for what it was. Lucifer arched one of his perfect brows. "Is that so?"

I marched away, needing distance from their prying eyes and that damn sword. Keeping my back to them, I took a deep breath and closed my eyes. Sending my awareness inside, I reached for what made me a demon. What made me a *vitium*. Dark and light. Good and evil.

My stomach burned as if I were famished, and a hollowness set up shop in my chest, encompassing the spot the sword had pierced. It grew until my upper body felt that blankness, that awful vacancy I'd experienced in the void. My mind fought it. My demon roared in warning.

I continued to push. To try and connect to that unknowable thing, yet the fear that I might wake it caused my limbs to shake harder and my bones to tremble. Cold sweat poured down my neck. A whisper of something evil spiraled up my spine.

I choked, the metallic taste of blood in my mouth. Someone shook me, and I jerked out of the darkness to find Lucifer gripping my arms and frowning down at me. The blood dribbled into my mouth as I gasped in a giant lungful of air.

Michael stood behind him, an identical frown on his face. "Did you see the artifacts?"

I shook my head. "I felt..."

"What?" Lucifer asked, releasing me.

Horrified? Terrified? I wiped the blood from under my nose with the back of my hand. "I need to be standing on the

Earth if I'm going to do this. The artifacts aren't here in the Lost City; they're on Earth. I can't find them from this plane. Also, I may need an amplifier."

Lucifer grunted in disapproval. "I don't want Azaria anywhere near these things, whatever they are."

"Kali's right," Michael countered. "The two of them together can do it." He now held the sword, and it flared brighter than it had previously. "One of The Omnis is right under our noses, and he's watching your every move, Kali. You can only scry for the artifacts under certain conditions when you're sure he can't sense you doing it or eavesdrop on your mind."

"Who?" Lucifer and I asked at the same time.

"Think about it." Michael tapped his temple. "He's been grooming you for a long time; you just didn't know it."

It was my turn to become wary. What had he said about these entities? They thrived on chaos and destruction. Chaos. "If you're going to tell me it's Rad, I'm gonna stop you right there. He may have been one of the Four Horsemen, but he's not one of The Omnis. I would know."

"Not him," Michael asserted. "The demon you've been with for centuries."

Lucifer sucked in a breath.

My stomach bottomed out. "No." It couldn't be.

There was some relief in the fact it wasn't my lover. Not Cole or Dru, either. But...

I shook my head adamantly. "You're wrong."

"I'm not." He held out the blade. "You're going to need this and Azaria. But for now, until we understand your new power and how to use it without tipping him off, you need to pretend everything is normal. Go back to your life as an investigator and Bridge employee. Don't let him even get a whiff of that essence inside you or what you're going to do with it, do you understand? If we tip our hand before we locate the artifacts, it's game over."

A part of me wondered if this was all another grand manipulation. Another game. Maybe Michael was controlling the sword to make us believe the lies he was feeding us. I couldn't wrap my mind around the idea that one of The Omnis was my friend and confidant. My mentor.

Oh, Damon.

The fact hit me in the gut all over again. He was an archdemon and so much more. I'd always thought the magic I felt from him was his incredible power, and it was—only that power wasn't solely demonic.

"You're sure?" I was proud of the way my voice didn't shake while I was falling apart inside. I directed the question to Michael, but a second meaning was directed at Lucifer. I hoped he understood my doubts and need for confirmation. "Sorry if I can't take your word for it. I need proof."

Faron and Bane appeared. "You need to return her before he becomes suspicious," Faron said to Michael. Then, to me, "He's going to interrogate you. You need to be prepared."

"Where have you been?" I couldn't keep the scorn out of my voice. "Don't think for one minute that I trust either of you."

"Likewise," Bane retorted, "but we're here to help."

"Like we did before," Faron added. "We know about The Omnis, and you'll need us moving forward."

Michael continued to hold out the sword. "They didn't skip out on you. They were making sure all the components came together for what happened. You were right about a few things—I was trying to save Tabriss. The only way to do that was to foil her agenda. I needed to know what she was planning, what her intentions were, to make sure she failed."

The blade flared.

Could I trust it?

"You don't seem all that upset that I caused her to explode."

Michael's face fell. "That was unfortunate. I didn't think it possible."

"None of us did," Faron said. "Not even Kali."

I took the weapon and pointed it at the Fate and her bodyguard as I glanced at Lucifer. "Do you believe them? Do you believe any of this that Michael is telling us?"

He didn't respond immediately, and his pause made all three of them uncomfortable. I felt his power reaching out to evaluate them individually but also sliding over me—not probing like it did to them, but soothing.

The stroke of his magic along my arms, over my shoulders, down my back, was uncomfortable and yet, wasn't. He was calming my demon, but also something else...

Angel. I'd heard the wards in Damon's private quarters whisper the word to me once. Now, it echoed in my brain again. *Angel, angel, angel.*

Blue light erupted from the sword, causing them to flinch and raise their hands to block the light from their eyes.

I swallowed hard. *It's only the remnants of Michael's essence.*

The blade dimmed.

A lie.

Lucifer lowered his hands and stared at me. "You can trust us. All of us."

In his words and in his eyes, I understood his true meaning—he recognized me now, or at least that part of me, as something akin to him. To Michael.

Angel.

My demon laughed. Evil was as much a part of me as anything. It wasn't buying into the angel bullshit, regardless of me being a *vitium*.

The handle of the sword warmed in my palm. "I'll search for the artifacts," I told them, "but I don't believe that Damon is one of The Omnis. Until I have proof, no one touches him, understand?"

If he was what they claimed, it would be me, and only me, who would end him.

28

*L*ucifer and I returned to chaos inside the Institute.

Lilith and Vicky had disappeared, taking dozens of demons with them. The fight between those who were left and the Fallen continued until Lucifer put a stop to it by incinerating the demons.

Many of the Fallen were injured. Damon put Di, Maddy, Kirill, and the other *vitiums* in charge of caring for them while Cole and his soldiers cleaned up the blood and guts left behind.

Lucifer ensured that Amy, Azaria, and their friends were again secured in the bunker. While Michael was no longer a threat, Lilith was still loose. No one was taking chances that she might launch a new campaign to eliminate Amy and the baby.

Zayfeer and Thesius appeared, and Lucifer brought them into the bunker with him. I avoided Damon, found Rad, and tasked him with hiding the sword in my apartment.

Then, I joined Cole in removing the demon ashes left behind in the training center.

Frank and Salmad were nowhere to be seen. A group of Fallen cornered me, demanding to know what had happened to Tabriss. I told them there had been an incident and that she wouldn't be coming back. They weren't satisfied with that answer, but Damon interrupted their cross-examination, sending them off to help care for their comrades.

Dru sought me out and asked if I was okay. I wasn't, and he could tell, but I lied and told him I was fine. He kissed my temple and told me he wanted the full story once I was rested. Damon caught my eye across the gymnasium and signaled me to follow him out.

Cole grunted. "You're getting called to the principal's office. Want company?"

He didn't ask why I had abandoned the fighting or what had happened on the roof. He didn't care about the Fallen, and Tabriss had been a pain in our ass since I'd brought her to the Institute. He was bruised and bleeding but in high spirits. War demons—brawling is their favorite thing.

"I appreciate the offer," I told him, brushing ash and goo from my pants. "But this debrief is going to be quick. Catch up with me later for a drink?"

"Count on it."

I picked my way through the debris, avoiding the splintered bleachers. The halls buzzed with conversations, and entities passed me here and there. Neve was in the elevator, the chihuahua in her lap, when it stopped to pick me up. "Are you all right?" she asked.

"Yes. You?"

The elevator began to move. "I've survived tornadoes, a

volcanic eruption, and an earthquake. None of them prepared me for this. Seriously, Kali, I don't know how you're still alive."

I chuckled as we stopped on Damon's floor. "I'm a demon, remember?"

"You're more than that, and you know it." Her gaze was serious as she wheeled herself out ahead of me. "I don't mean physically. I'm talking about mentally and emotionally."

My emotions were stuffed into a bottomless, very dark hole. My mind was a mess, and I was trying to clear it before confronting Damon. The fact he could often read my thoughts, regardless if I had shields in place, unnerved me more than I wanted to admit. If he got a whiff of the fact I suspected him of being an Omni, it was game over. "I suppose I should start meditating like you. It would probably help."

She shifted the dog so she could pull a crystal from her pocket. The light reflected off it, the soft blue the same color as the flames of Michael's sword. "This is angelite. I find it to be very calming."

Angels. Bleh.

She handed it to me, and I rolled it around in my palm. The energy was deceptive—it packed a wallop of serenity and tranquility. Instantly, the racing thoughts in my head settled.

She dug out another, offering it to me as well. "This is labradorite. It's protective, especially with your empathy and intuition. It will keep other people's thoughts and emotions from overwhelming you."

When I held that stone up, it flashed distinctively gold and green. "Will it stop others from reading my mind?"

Her eyes narrowed. "It can't hurt. Do we have mind readers here now?"

I glanced toward Damon's closed door. "At times." I smiled at her. "Thank you for these."

She took off down the hall, and I faced the door. Before I could raise my hand to knock, Damon barked, "Get in here."

I tunneled into my magic, slid my shields into place, swaggered in, and plopped down on his sofa.

He'd expected me to take the seat across from him and swiveled my direction and waited. When I didn't immediately start talking, he lifted an eyebrow and gave me *the look*. The one that told me to start talking.

"What is it you want to know?" I asked. "You were there. You heard it all."

He studied me, searching my face. "You disappeared from the roof with Lucifer. Where did you go? What happened?"

This was where it got tricky. Rather than relaying the blow-by-blow details, which I couldn't do without revealing our suspicions, I gave him an abbreviated version of the current situation. "Michael tried to outsmart us, but his machinations have only resulted in him being banned from Heaven. God isn't happy with him right now. The angel Thelesis can confirm that. He's my—"

"I know who and what he is." That intense scrutiny prodded my shields. He made no qualms about the attempt either. *Rude.* "You spoke true, then, about Michael sabotaging the prophecy to save Tabriss?"

I shoved his jabbing magic away. "He knew they could never be together, but he didn't want to see her annihilated."

"I imagine he was furious after you did exactly that to her."

This was safer territory. "About that... Michael and I discussed it, and I'm not sure exactly how that happened or why."

"Sal is distraught."

"Sal can go to Hell."

He rocked in his seat. The probing stopped. "Where will Michael go?"

"Don't know, don't care."

Lucifer popped in. "I would ask for sanctuary for him here."

"Here?" I scoffed, hiding my relief at his appearance and request. Took the spotlight off me. "You can't be serious."

I knew he was. His new plan was to insert Michael into the Institute to keep an eye on Damon. Lucifer, too, would now have a reason to hang around with his family safely ensconced in the underground bunker.

Damon appeared unruffled. "Why would we do that? He has presented as a serious enemy to us."

"You have my word that he's no longer your enemy or mine." Lucifer used his *don't forget your place* voice that made my demon tremble. "In exchange for room and board, he will assist us in tracking down and rehabilitating the rest of the Fallen. If he causes even an ounce of trouble, I'll deal with him myself."

Damon's gaze slid to me. His face was unreadable, but I knew he was suspicious. Whether it was of me or Lucifer, I wasn't sure. "Is this acceptable to you?"

"Hell, no," I said, pouring the old Kali into my act. She would never have accepted such an arrangement, and I gave an indignant huff. "Stick him in that apartment you rented for me," I told Lucifer. "We don't want him here."

"How do we know he has truly been banned from Heaven?" Damon questioned Lucifer. "Do you have proof, or are you simply accepting his word about it?"

Lucifer stood his ground, looking down his nose at us in his typical, arrogant manner. "The gates are locked, and Thelesis confirms that Michael can no longer pass through them."

Damon seemed to think this over. "I'm not in the habit of opening my doors to my enemies, but I can see there may be a benefit to keeping him under our watchful eye."

Continuing my act, I came to my feet, hands going to my hips. "No way. You can't let him in here after everything he's done!"

Scorching heat hit me, and I glanced at Lucifer. He thought I was overdoing it. I almost snickered. He had no idea. "I cannot bind his power, but there are ways for us to ensure he has limited access to certain areas of the Institute, such as your personal quarters," he assured Damon. "He needs to be near my daughter because he is still her protector, so he will spend most of his time in the bunker. I'll let you decide where else he is allowed to go. It would be good for him to be able to use the training center, but the weapons can be off-limits."

Damon nodded, no longer concerned with my resistance. He was all about strategy and what might benefit the Institute. Now, I was suspicious. He was planning to use Michael for something... "What is the plan going forward to retrieve the other Fallen scattered across the Earth?" he asked Lucifer.

"Gabriel and Michael will take charge of that," Lucifer informed him. "I will find locations in each country for the Fallen to be housed and trained. Many of those you've helped will be assigned to the houses to take up leadership positions there and ensure the new Fallen are well cared for during their rehabilitation."

I dropped back down on the sofa, exhausted. I used this to act exasperated about Michael moving in, but I was relieved. It was a brilliant master plan that would take some of the heat off me.

"And us?" Damon asked. "Do you still require us to help?"

"Only as a way station or temporary sanctuary as we move them around. Your job now is to hunt down the demons who have escaped, along with Lilith. She needs to be returned to her rightful position in Hell."

Another nod from my boss. "Kali will get right on it. That is"—he flicked an unconcerned glance at me—"she's again my employee."

"I'm happy to return her," Lucifer said with a bit too much enthusiasm.

"Good." Damon sat forward and opened a file. "You can start today."

"Today?" I glared at him. "How about a little time off? I've been going nonstop for months."

He closed the file as if it were a monumental effort to indulge me. "You start on Monday," he ordered. "Get some rest."

I was effectively dismissed, and it was all I could do to

hide my joy as I moped my way to the door, casting back a snide glance at the two of them. "I'll look for Lilith, but I want equal time to handle cases for Sweet Investigations. I need some balance in my life."

"The sooner we send Lilith back to Hell, the better," Lucifer insisted.

"I agree," Damon said, "but Kali's right—she needs to attend to her business. She has quite a backlog, and those cases may lead her to the escaped demons, who, in turn, will assist us in tracking down Lilith."

It was total logic, but I flashed a quick, grateful smile. "Exactly."

"Fine," Lucifer grumbled.

"Fine," I snapped back.

I didn't bother shutting the door on my way out, allowing the grin to break free once I was in the elevator.

29

*R*ad waited for me in my apartment. I leaped into his arms, and he kissed me thoroughly. All the tension I'd been holding washed out of me. I allowed myself a moment to relax.

He set me away from him, tracing his fingers over my belly. "Is it true? What you said about Michael... You were never pregnant with his child?"

"Oh, hell no." I didn't see any point in telling him it had been a real scare for me for a few minutes. "That was a purposeful misdirection. He did stick some of his angel mojo in me, but I'm baby-free, and thank the fires of Hell for that."

A mixture of relief and something else—sadness?— passed over his face. "I wouldn't have cared, you know. Archangel or no, you belong to me. You and your baby would belong to me."

I stroked a finger down his cheek and stared at his perfection. He was handsome in the way of Greek gods. "You make it sound like I'm your property."

"You're my mate, and while the idea of another male touching you or even looking at you enrages me, where you go, I go. You are mine to protect and care for, even though you don't want me to."

"I don't *need* you to. There's a difference." I brushed a kiss over his lips, pressing his solid firmness. "I like it when you're like this," I teased. "All territorial and dominant."

He nipped my bottom lip. "Good thing since I don't intend to change."

"I have good news."

He stroked my hair, tipping my head back and searching my eyes. "I'm listening."

"My only job for the Bridge Institute right now is to search for Lilith. I can go back to Sweet Investigations part-time while I do that."

"What about the Fallen?"

"Lucifer and Damon are working out a deal, but Lucifer has enlisted other help and no longer needs me."

"What happened when you disappeared with him? Where did you go?"

I planned to tell him everything, regardless of the fact that Lucifer and Michael wanted me to keep it a secret. I needed to tell him about The Omnis. Like he said, we were partners, soulmates, and I wasn't going to keep something that important from him. I'd done stuff like that before, but not anymore.

The only thing holding me back was that we were still inside the Institute. I was still too close to Damon and his mind-reading abilities.

Putting physical distance between us might not be enough to break that, but I had a few ideas on how to work around it. The Lost City would come into play, and the ring I wore around my neck would be my access key to it. I just needed Lucifer to rewire the magic, so it took me there rather than here.

For now, all I wanted was to indulge in what every demon wants—food, sex, and sleep. "Pack your things. We're going home. I have a lot to tell you."

He sauntered to the closet and drew out a distressed leather satchel and a guitar case. "I'm ready."

"You're packed?" I pointed at the bag. "That's it?"

"All I need is you." He hefted it up. "This bag is yours."

He unzipped it, and I peered inside. Volante was curled at the bottom. "It seemed to understand that I needed to disguise it, and it morphed into your whip."

I stroked the coiled leather, and it immediately responded. Like the real Volante, this one curled around my arm and settled there with an audible sigh. The sword acted so much like her that I wasn't sure it hadn't absorbed her sentience somehow. Either way, this was the best disguise ever.

He tossed the empty bag back into the closet and grabbed my hand. "Let's get out of this place."

At home in my church, the structure seemed too quiet and empty after the past months at the busy, overflowing Institute. I stood in my sunken living room, soaking it in and sending my magic into all of the supports, foundation, and walls. The place responded immediately, sending back tendrils of its inherent magic, welcoming me home.

Rad and I gorged ourselves on what food we could find, ordered in more, and made love while we waited for it to be delivered. We slept for twelve hours, woke, ate, and talked.

Sunrise found us on the roof with espressos in hand, watching the first light of day spread across the landscape. It lined the cemetery's edges, where the ghosts stared back at us. Even they seemed relieved that I was home.

"Have you ever wanted kids?" I asked him, my fingers intertwined with his. The sadness I'd seen on his face when I told him I wasn't pregnant had made me wonder.

He shrugged one shoulder, sipping the last of his drink. "Even if I could reproduce, I would make a terrible father."

"I don't think so."

He shot me an inquisitive look.

"I think you'd be good at it. Far better than me at parenting, anyway."

He chuckled. "This world is so screwed up, I'd end up trying to put them in a bubble."

"Me, too. There's hope, though. When the Fallen are rehabilitated and set loose in the world, I believe they'll reverse much of the fear and destruction that has been going on since the fall of Paradise."

"Do you really believe there's a new world coming?"

"I'm as jaded as they come, but yeah. I actually do."

"Then maybe we should discuss having kids again one of these days."

My heart gave a little twist. What kind of entity would we create, even if I could get pregnant? There was no guarantee that I'd be able to. Not only was he equal parts human and chaos demon, I was a bloody mess of too many things. "I'd like that."

"You would?"

It was definitely a New World Order if I was considering having children. Yet, I found the idea intriguing. Holding

Azaria and feeling the spark in my belly that I'd initially believed was a child had shifted my ideas.

AT NINE ON MONDAY MORNING, I let myself into my office. Sophie was aware of my presence, flicking on the lights and greeting me as I entered.

"How many cases do we have?" I asked as I sat at my desk with a cup of coffee.

"Two active ones that Di and Maddy are working on," she responded. "There are four-hundred and twenty-three requests for your assistance, as well."

I spit coffee on the blotter and hurriedly searched for a napkin to wipe it up. "I'm sorry. Could you repeat that? It sounded like you said four hundred and twenty-three potential clients need my services."

"That's correct," she responded. A series of lists and spreadsheets appeared on the giant screens across the room from me. "I have categorized them according to their issue and the supernatural parties involved. Where would you like to start?"

My tech guru, JR, poked his head in. "You're back."

He typically did not meet anyone's eyes when he spoke, but when I glanced at him, he looked directly at me and smiled. "I am. We have a lot of work to do. Grab your tablet and take a seat."

The grin grew, and he disappeared. "Be right back," he called.

Di and Maddy showed up next, the dog tucked under the vampire's arm. Milena wore a jacket with tulips and rainbows on it. Di handed me a bag of donuts she'd purchased from the coffee shop down the street. They were still warm. I dug in.

"Sophie said you needed us." Maddy set the dog on the ground, and Milly began sniffing around.

"We have a no-dog policy," I said.

Di grabbed a donut with sprinkles and crossed her legs after she sank onto the sofa. "We absolutely do not."

The dog ran to her and began begging for a piece of her treat. She happily supplied it, creating a bed beside her on the cushion with the quilt left from one of my previous overnight stays.

JR returned, grabbing a glazed donut before sitting. "Okay, boss. What's first?"

Maddy slumped into the other visitor's chair, texting someone. "I need coffee."

She reached for my cup, but I snatched it away. "Get your own."

Ever the drama queen, she rolled her eyes so hard her head flipped back before she sauntered off to do just that.

An hour later, the four of us had a game plan to close out the two open cases and start on the new client list. There were several I wanted to turn over to the Bridge and its enforcer, but the majority I was keeping.

Even as I sat there, Sophia and JR took more calls requesting our assistance. Damon had been right—the loose demons were terrorizing my city.

I met Rad for lunch and handed him the cases that fell under the Bridge's jurisdiction. I also alerted him to the most pressing ones on my plate that might be related to the recent rash of new demons in our area. He could pass on the information to Damon, and I would wait for the archdemon to decide which he wanted my input on, if any.

I started with the ones closest to my office, checking off several before I stopped at the Chicago House to talk to Dru. He welcomed me into his den, drawing me in close and breathing deeply, his nose close to my neck. "You smell different."

"I imagine so." I eased away. Was it the piece of The Unknowing I'd absorbed? "I've been dancing between planes of existence, got shot with angel magic, and had a vampire's sword driven into my chest. It's been a rough few days."

"Hmm." He poured me a glass of wine from his bar cart and gestured for me to sit on the couch beside him. I did, sipping the wine and hoping he didn't ask for specifics.

Of course, he did. "There's more to it than that, isn't there? You know I'm here if you wish to discuss it. I'm quite curious as to what Lucifer has been forcing you to do for him."

I settled the glass on the coffee table and leaned back to study his face. "If I didn't know better, I'd say that's jealousy in your tone. You don't really think I have something going on with Lucifer Morningstar, do you?"

He reached over and teased a finger down my leather-clad thigh. "Something *is* going on between the two of you. He has his hooks in you. I don't like it."

He sure did, and I didn't like it either. "I'm working on removing them, but it will take time and cleverness on my part."

"Do tell."

"Once I have a solid plan, I'll share it with you. For now,

I'm staying as far away from him and the Institute as possible. I'm searching for Lilith and Vicky. Have you gotten wind of either?"

Changing the subject didn't please him, but he nodded. "I have several leads for you, but I also have a request."

"Go on."

"Vicky is one of my nest. Although she has violated many of our covenants, she is my responsibility. Yours, as well. Her connection to Lilith cannot be denied, but once we find her, you and I will decide together on her punishment. Agreed?"

Saying 'no' would only lead to an argument, and as queen of the Chicago vampires, I had certain responsibilities and obligations to him and the House. He was within his right to request this. "Agreed, and if you are available, I could use your help hunting Lilith."

He grinned, and the vampire in him shone in his eyes. "Thought you'd never ask."

When I returned to SI, the day was done. Di, Maddy, and JR were still working, but I sent them on their respective ways. "We reconvene tomorrow at nine, like usual."

They said their goodbyes. I kicked up my heels on the desk, and Sophia brought up my favorite playlist. Rad texted asking about dinner, and I sent a reply. Tossing the phone down, I eased back in my chair and smiled.

I still had plenty on my plate, but I'd done it. I'd saved the world. Saved my friends from total annihilation.

And then Faron materialized, startling the crap out of me.

I jerked my feet off the desk. "What are you doing here?"

She sank into a chair. "I need a job."

"Bully for you. The shop down the road is hiring."

She shot me a rebellious look. "Not just any job. Some-thing...useful."

I rocked back, considering why she would be here sharing this with me. "Lucifer fired you."

She shrugged. "He doesn't need my services now. No one does, I guess."

Damon had taught me to use every opportunity, even those that on the surface looked like problems, to my advan-tage. With her skill set, she could be useful. For Sweet Inves-tigations and for figuring out whether Damon was more than he seemed. "How do you feel about becoming a demon bounty hunter? There aren't actual bounties to be paid, but I offer a competitive wage and a few benefits."

Mostly free coffee and occasional donuts, but...

"I'll take it." She stood. "When do I start?"

"Sophie?"

"Yes, mistress?"

"Add Faron to the payroll."

"Done. Will she be signing her noncompete agreement by pen or with blood?"

Faron blinked. "Uh...pen?"

"Printing a paper copy now," Sophie said.

Faron hiked a thumb over her shoulder at the screen. "Mistress?"

"Yes," I said. "This is my domain. What about your bodyguard?"

"He's waiting in the parking lot."

Hmm. I retrieved the agreement and handed it and a pen to her. "This offer isn't a package deal."

"I know, but he can be useful."

Another opportunity? "I'll consider him a subcontractor for now, but if he steps out of line..."

She scribbled her name on the line and slid the paper across the desktop. "I won't let him."

"Sophie will send you a list of cases to start with. We have a lot on our docket right now."

"How many is a lot?"

"Four hundred and twenty-nine," Sophie supplied.

The number just kept going up.

Bang... Bang... Bang...

They were dull, slow knocks at the back door. Faron and I turned.

In the next round, there were only two, and my sensitive ears picked up the sound of ragged crying.

"Sophie, show me the view of the back door."

The screen flashed with a scene that made me stand.

A *trick*, my demon insisted.

Was it?

Faron shifted her gaze between me and the screen. "Do you want me to answer it?"

I studied the person on the threshold—the blood, the burn marks. The way she slumped against the building, barely able to raise her arm to knock.

Shield locked in place, I marched down the hall. "Sophie, scan the parking lot and nearby area for signs of potential threats."

My heart beat twice before she said, "Thermal imaging shows two birds, various insects, and two hybrid supernatural creatures. One is a vampire-witch. The other is unknown."

"Bane," Faron said. "But he's not a threat."

Guess we'd see about that.

My options were to leave Vicky on my back doorstep and let her die or take a risk and open the door.

I owed her nothing, yet I was still connected to her. "Send a message to Master Vampire Dru that I've found Victoria. Inform him she's here, and he should come and get her."

"Sending message now," she replied.

"Do you want me to let Bane handle her?" Faron asked.

"I can handle her." I opened the door, and Vicky, propped against it, flopped across the threshold at my feet.

Her curly red hair had been singed off. Burns covered most of the visible skin. Her eyelashes were gone, lips blackened. The clothes she wore had melted to her body, and blood leaked from her ears, nose, and an assortment of cuts on her hands and stomach. "Help," she whispered.

There was no good way to pull her inside, so I made it as quick as possible, her screams echoing in my ears. I slammed the door shut and locked it, leaning against it as she whimpered on the cool tiles.

"Damn," Faron uttered. "What happened to her?"

"Lilith," I told the Fate. To Vicky, I said, "Hate to say I told you so, but I told you so. If you play with her, she's going to burn you."

She coughed and wheezed. "She tried to...kill me."

Even in her state of horrible pain, her voice was filled with shock that the queen of demons would do such a thing.

I was no healer, but my magic could ease her pain until her vampire blood kicked in and did it. It would take some time, but she would live, thanks to that very blood combined with what she'd taken from me when we'd first met.

Learning the person you idolized would betray you sucked. I rolled the labradorite around in my pocket as I assessed her injuries. The fact that I had empathy for the hybrid astounded me, but I did. "You survived, and you'll heal."

She reached out a hand and grabbed my leg. "That's... not...enough."

I disengaged her grip, which was easy enough to do since she was so weak. "What do you want?"

Her black lips curled back in a cruel smile filled with malice. "Revenge," she hissed.

Such a strange chain of events. "Well," I said, smiling down at her. "I happen to be an expert at that."

She sighed, slumping down and closing her eyes. "You're...hired."

And just like that, client number four hundred and thirty was added to my list.

VISIT MY STORE

Did you know you can buy directly from me? When you do, the retailer doesn't take a cut and I can pass on the savings to YOU!

https://mistyevansbooks.com/shop

Benefits:

You can find ALL my books in one place

SAVE money

EARLY access to new releases

Special Collections, Boxed Sets, and Limited Editions

Support a small business (and support a dream!)

Why Buy Direct?

When you purchase a book by your favorite author, electronic or print, on retailer platforms, the company keeps 30-70% of the sale, leaving the author with little to no profit (after the company deducts delivery fees, taxes, and other fees).

Buying directly from the author means that more goes to them so they can keep turning out stories for you. Every published story, every book, requires cover art, editing, and hours and hours of the author's time simply to create it. Not to mention overhead costs, such as websites, newsletters, writing software, graphics programs, advertising, taxes, etc.

In addition, one of the big-name retailers requires exclusivity, and all of them have terms of service and rules and regulations that make it challenging and time-consuming for an indie author to navigate the publishing world.

Most of us would MUCH rather spend our time creating more stories for YOU, rather than trying to jump through the hoops at the retailers. Buying direct from your favorite authors (where available) helps ensure that an author you love is not subject to unexplained account closures, withholding of royalties, censorship, and other issues that can affect their livelihood.

I've experienced ALL of these. By buying direct, you help put control of my work back in my hands - and I can continue to write more.

Either way, thank you for supporting me! I understand buying direct doesn't work for everyone and even if you use the retailers to buy my books, I appreciate you!

Happy reading,

Misty

https://mistyevansbooks.com/shop

YOU'RE INVITED!

Do you have a passion for my stories?
Want more from my characters?
How about early access to ALL my new releases?
My reader community is for YOU!

Try my **Magic Bites reader community** for a month! It's ONLY $5 - you're buying me a coffee - and in return, you get all these perks:

　✦ **Writing Updates** so you know what's in the works and how soon you can get it

　✦ **Special Content,** including chapters in new and upcoming stories

　✦ **FREE Access to new books** - Read all of my new urban fantasy releases for FREE before they're available at retailers

Don't miss out on this opportunity! Join my Magic Bites reader community today.

I'm in! Give me more stories!

PNR & UF BY MISTY/NYX HALLIWELL

The Accidental Reaper Series

Grim & Bare It, Book 1

Reaper's Keepers, Book 2

In too Reap, Book 3

Killin' It (short story for newsletter subscribers only)

The Vampire's Kiss (an exclusive short story available in Misty's Store. *Intended for mature audiences 17+*)

Grave Girl

Grave Magic

Grim Vows

The Kali Sweet Series

Revenge Is Sweet, Kali Sweet Series, Book 1

Sweet Chaos, Kali Sweet Series, Book 2

Sweet Soldier, Kali Sweet Series, Book 3

Sweet Curse, Kali Sweet Series, Book 4

Sweet Malice, Book 5

Sweet Betrayal, Book 6 (coming 2026)

Witches Anonymous Step 1

Jingle Hells, WA Step 2

Wicked Souls, WA Step 3

Dark Moon Lilith, Witches Anonymous Step 4

Dancing With the Devil, Witches Anonymous Step 5

Devil's Due, Witches Anonymous Step 6

Dirty Deeds, Witches Anonymous Step 7

Wicked Wedding, Witches Anonymous Step 8

～

Soul Survivor, Moon Water Series, Book 1

Soul Protector, Moon Water Series, Book 2

～

COZY MYSTERIES (WRITING AS NYX HALLIWELL)

Sister Witches Of Raven Falls Mystery Series

Of Potions and Portents

Of Curses and Charms

Of Stars and Spells

Of Spirits and Superstition

～

Confessions of a Closet Medium Series

Pumpkins & Poltergeists

Magic & Mistletoe

Hearts & Haunts

Vows & Vengeance

Cupcakes & Corpses

Tea Leaves & Troubled Spirits

Haunted Honeymoon

Wedding Bells & Psychic Spells

Phantoms Are Forever

Sister Witches of Story Cove Series

Cinder

Belle

Snow

Ruby

Zelle

Sister Witches of Story Cove Complete Set

***

Witchy Candy Shop Mysteries

Tricks and Treats

Candy and Creeps

Gum and Ghouls (releasing 2025)

THRILLING ROMANTIC SUSPENSE & MYSTERIES

Don't want to miss a single release? Click here to join my reader list!

Black Swan Division Romantic Thriller Series

Redeeming Meg

Tempting Tessa

Avenging Jessie

SEALs of Shadow Force Series

Fatal Truth

Fatal Honor

Fatal Courage

Fatal Love

Fatal Vision

Fatal Thrill

Risk

SEALS of Shadow Force Series: Spy Division

Man Hunt

Man Killer

Man Down

Covert Affairs

Covert Tactics

Covert Obsession

The SCVC Taskforce Series

Deadly Pursuit

Deadly Deception

Deadly Force

Deadly Intent

Deadly Affair, A SCVC Taskforce novella

Deadly Attraction

Deadly Secrets

Deadly Holiday, A SCVC Taskforce novella

Deadly Target

Deadly Rescue

Deadly Bounty

Deadly Betrayal

Deadly Threat

The Super Agent Series

Operation Sheba

Operation Paris

Operation Proof of Life

Operation Lost Princess

Operation Ambush

Operation Contraband

Operation Sleeping With the Enemy

Operation Heist

The Justice Team Series (with Adrienne Giordano)

Stealing Justice

Cheating Justice

Holiday Justice

Exposing Justice

Undercover Justice

Protecting Justice

Missing Justice

Defending Justice

SCHOCK SISTERS MYSTERY SERIES w/Adrienne Giordano

1st Shock

2nd Strike

3rd Tango

∼

The Secret Ingredient Culinary Mystery Series

The Secret Ingredient, A Culinary Romantic Mystery with Bonus Recipes

The Secret Life of Cranberry Sauce, A Secret Ingredient Holiday Novella

MEET MISTY

USA TODAY Bestselling Author Misty Evans has published nearly one hundred fiction novels. She loves writing urban fantasy, paranormal romance, and mystery/suspense. Under her pen name, Nyx Halliwell, she also writes supernatural cozy mysteries.

When not reading or writing, she enjoys music, movies, and hanging out with her husband, twin sons, and three spoiled rescue dogs. She's a crafter at heart and has far too many projects to finish.

Visit www.mistyevansbooks.com to check out her online store and sign up for her newsletter.

LETTER FROM MISTY

Hello Beautiful Reader!

Thank you for reading this story! It is an honor and a privilege to write books for you. I'm an indie author and every fan is important to me. I pour my heart into each story and do my best to bring you an escape from the real world.

Readers are the key to my success - not a traditional publishing deal (had four), an agent (had two), or a publicity team (yep, you guessed it, had several of those as well.)

Those of you who read my books, love my characters and worlds, and then tell others about them are the best of friends. I adore you and will keep writing if you keep reading!

If you'd like to learn about my other books, sales, and special promotions, please sign up for my newsletter at **www.mistyevansbooks.com.**

You'll get coupons to download starter packs for FREE, whether you love my suspense or my paranormal.

Support me directly (no retailer taking their cut), grab special edition box sets, and get new releases before they are out at retailers by visiting my store **https://mistyevansbooks. com/shop.**

I have sales and offer NEW RELEASES early! Check it out.

Last but not least, if you enjoy clean, cozy mysteries, visit my pen name **www.nyxhalliwell.com** to see those books.

Thank you, and happy reading!

Misty